Juked

EDITOR

RYAN RIDGE

FICTION EDITOR

ASHLEY FARMER

POETRY EDITORS

MICHAEL BARACH
COLLIER NOGUES

ASSOCIATE EDITORS

CHRISTY CRUTCHFIELD
WILL DONNELLY
HARRIS LAHTI
BOBBY RICH

COVER DESIGN

CLAIRE KRUEGER

PUBLISHER

JOHN WEI HAN WANG

ISBN: 978-0-9973972-3-9

Read more at www.juked.com.
You can reach us at info@juked.com, or at:

Juked
108 New Mark Esplanade
Rockville, MD 20850

TABLE OF CONTENTS

NONFICTION

FICTION

POETRY

LEAVING WINTER

The thing about winter is that in a practical sense it no longer exists for me. In November of 2015, less than a week before Thanksgiving, Kristen and I packed up our house in Rhode Island and moved to California. Our son Max, our cat Bunny, and I flew with my mother, who had helped us pack, while Kristen and her father drove our car from one side of the country to the other.

Things turned strange almost immediately. This is often the case with Kristen and I when we travel, particularly if it is a trip of some importance. The first time I flew out to see her, when we were first dating, I sat directly behind a young Indian woman who confessed to her row-mate before takeoff that 1) this was her first flight and that 2) her asthma inhaler had been taken away at security. About two hours into the flight I noticed the seat shaking in front of me. I looked up from my book to realize that the woman was having trouble breathing. The more she worried about it, the more difficulty she had. The woman seated next to her, by coincidence, was a nurse. "Breathe through your nose, honey, breathe through your nose," she kept saying in a remarkably calm and placid voice. The Indian woman's eyes were closed, so she couldn't see the remarkable contrast between the calmness of the nurse's voice and the terror on her blanched face. *She believes this woman might die*, I realized. A cylinder of oxygen was opened and a mask strapped over the Indian woman's face, which seemed to do little to help. A desperate search was made through the plane for another inhaler, and then suddenly we were making an emergency landing in Traverse City, Michigan. As a result, I missed my connection in Minneapolis, spent the night in a cheap motel, and showed up to meet the woman I would end up marrying a day late.

This time, Kristen's father had misread his ticket, so when Kristen called to see if he was about to take off, she discovered he was still sitting at home in Idaho, three hours away from the Salt Lake airport. He would make it, but would arrive a day late.

In addition, with everything packed and on the moving van, we suddenly couldn't find Bunny. He was simply gone, and we managed to convince ourselves that he was hiding in the space under our basement stairs — there was a hole just big enough for him to get in. The commotion from the movers, we thought, had been enough to drive him into hiding. We looked outside although we were convinced there hadn't been an opportunity for him to leave. We opened a can of cat food and left it out near the stairs. We called to him repeatedly and listened, heard nothing. We left, then came back, but the food was untouched. Had he managed to get into our attic crawlspace somehow? We opened that up, called out, but still no sign of Bunny.[1]

When we signed over the mortgage, we explained to the new owners that our cat was lost in the house. They had a dog, they told us, so probably the dog would find him. We had visions of our cat being torn to pieces by their dog, which didn't seem like an auspicious way for us to leave our house, and an even less auspicious way for them to start living in it. They tried to reassure us: they were planning to do some work on the house, so wouldn't be moving in for almost a month. Which meant, I suppose, our cat had a better chance of starving to death than being torn apart by their dog.

We begged them to let us hang onto the key for a few more hours. While my mother and I took Max to his final swim lesson, Kristen went back but still couldn't find Bunny. She worked her

---

[1] I'd already had problems with Bunny on this trip. When I'd first arranged for Bunny to fly with me, I had gone through the whole process of reserving a place for him on Southwest Airlines. Everything had gone remarkably smoothly until the moment the operator said, "Well, we're all set then, Jenny," and I realized that she'd somehow crossed my ticket with someone else's, and thought I was a remarkably low-voiced woman.

arm back as far as she could under the stairs and with her phone took a series of pictures. From these, it was clear that Bunny wasn't there.

So where was he? She called out his name again, then listened, then called again.

And then she heard him meow. It was distant and hard to hear and for a moment she searched the basement frantically for other hiding spaces that we'd perhaps neglected, before realizing that Bunny was outside. He was standing in our backyard beside the shed, waiting patiently. Somehow during the move, he had managed to sneak out. Probably he had even found someone to feed him.

As a result of all that, Max, Bunny, my mother, and I almost missed our flight. In addition, Kristen and her father started driving about a day and a half later than they'd planned, on November 20th. It was clear by now that they would hit snow, but they figured they'd drive as far as possible the first day and then take a little longer on the later part of the trip if they needed. Kristen would meet me in Utah, then we'd drive together (along with Max—we'd leave Bunny at my parents' place) to my sister's house in Santa Monica, where she and Max would live until the house we were buying in Valencia closed, hopefully, in early December. Meanwhile, almost immediately after Thanksgiving, I would fly back to Rhode Island to teach my final classes at Brown University.

They discussed whether to take a southern route instead of heading across on I-80 as they had originally planned, but the amount of time they would lose seemed to outweigh the advantages. Besides, Kristen's dad had been a salesman covering a large territory—he'd spent a good chunk of his life on the road, and he lived in Eastern Idaho, so was used to winter weather. He liked to drive, loved road trips—which was one of the reasons that Kristen had wanted to do the trip with him. That and because it seemed unimaginable to spend five days on the road with our then-two-year-old son and a cat.

They set off. They would, they decided, drive long days and try to make it to Utah in time for Thanksgiving. But after they'd driven only a few hours they began to get word that the storm was likely to be worse than originally predicted.

They stopped in Erie, Pennsylvania and slept there, leaving early the next day. On November 20th and 21st, Chicago received 11.2" of snow, almost double the amount of snow they'd ever had for the first storm of the year. A layer of ice built up on the road. As Kristen and her dad got closer to Chicago, visibility became worse and worse. They kept passing semi-trucks that had jacknifed and turned over or had simply slid off the road. A thick crust of ice had built up on the hood of the car — a Prius: not the most practical car for snow-driving, as it turns out — making it hard to see. The radio was telling people to get off the highway, but every time they came to an exit, the confusion off the highway seemed more intense than what they were facing on the now-nearly-deserted road. Illinois, unlike Kansas, doesn't have gates that can be used to block the highway off, so there was nothing but black ice and driving to keep them from continuing on. Kristen was driving, despite the fact that she hates to drive under stressful circumstances. Every time they passed a disabled truck, its load spilled out, her dad would say, "There's somebody who lost his job." They were trying to call ahead to figure out where they could get a hotel, her dad talking loudly into the earpiece he always keeps in his ear except when he sleeps (and sometimes even then), but they kept striking out.

Then the low coolant light came on. Something was happening with the car that made it so it would only go into gas-powered mode, not electric, and so it sounded like it was constantly revving, as if the engine was in distress or wouldn't come out of low gear.

This had happened to us once before, just about a month prior, right after we'd taken the car in for service, when we were on our way to Boston Logan to fly out to California to look for a house. While I drove, Kristen read online that this was an indication of a serious malfunction and that we should take the car to the dealership immediately. But we couldn't do so without missing our flight. I kept driving, expecting the car to die at any moment, but we made it to the airport.

The Southern California real estate market turned out to be radically different from Rhode Island: we were leaving a buyer's market to enter a seller's one. The day before flying out, we'd chosen a dozen houses to look at, but by the time our plane landed, more than half of those houses were under contract. We looked quickly through the remainder. One seemed nice enough, but was about half the size of our previous home. Another was great if you could ignore the fact that it had an active termite infestation. We adjusted our expectations and our price range and found a house in a neighborhood we liked, but the house itself seemed to have been decorated by someone who was an interior designer for midwestern Mexican restaurants — including artificially-induced smoke stains on the walls. We made an offer on that house, even though our realtor tried to talk us out of it. That offer was turned down.

So, Kristen ended up going street by street through the neighborhoods we wanted to live in until she found a house we hadn't seen. It had been on the market for three weeks — a long time in that market — but had been mislisted: the man selling the house had decided to go with a realtor from his church who had been out of the market for twenty years, and who didn't know about things like Zillow and Trulia so hadn't listed the house online. They were panicking because they'd had no offers. We made an offer, and got the house.

There's more to this sub-story, but it's worth saving for another essay, one that's not ostensibly about winter. For instance, our realtor's husband had a backpack heart, an experimental heart that since has been discontinued because of the fact that it had a tendency to inexplicably fail.[2] Someone had to be with her

---

[2] Which indeed her husband's did in the parking lot of Costco, giving her ninety seconds as an alarm screeched to dig out and attach a backup battery,

husband 24 hours a day in case his heart failed, so a pair of friends trained in how to change his heart battery were watching him when she took us shopping for houses. She asked us over lunch at what would become our favorite Mexican restaurant (despite it looking remarkably like the house we had made the offer on) if it would be okay to bring her backpack-hearted husband along next time. With both of us being writers, what else could we say but yes? Which meant that he was there when we looked at the house we ended up buying, his backpack heart making a loud swishing noise as the dog in the backyard barked at him. "Henri! Henri!" our realtor yelled at him. "Your heart is scaring the dog! Go inside!" This, as much as anything about the house itself, probably was what convinced us it was the right house for us.

When we flew back to Boston after finding our house, I was convinced we would need to have our car towed the forty-five miles back to Providence. But the car started, exhibiting that same overburdened revving, and so I drove it home, suspecting I was doing irrevocable harm to the engine. It was snowing outside, the road wet and slick. But we made it home and the next day I drove it to the dealership—it didn't die on the way there either. They claimed the radiator fluid was low and suggested the cap must have been left a little loose after the service, so they topped it off and told us we were fine.

But obviously we were not fine—or rather Kristen was not fine, since she was in the middle of the country in a snowstorm having the same problem. A lot of ice had built up on the grill of the car—maybe that was blocking something? Maybe they could just top the radiator off again and it'd last for another thousand miles? The next day was Sunday, which meant it would be difficult to have the car looked at.

They slept at a hotel in Joliet, topped off the radiator the next

---

which she managed to do.

day, knocked off the ice and kept driving. At first it seemed like the problem was solved, and then the light came on again and the revving resumed. Maybe, we speculated, the dealership had forgotten to reset some of the codes, and if they just could get that done the car would no longer rev and drive like normal? They stopped at a truck stop and a mechanic there volunteered to turn off the signal, but then it turned out he didn't have the proper code. It was still snowing, the roads still awful. Because of what was going on with the car they could only go so fast, but because of road conditions they could only go so fast anyway. They drove on to Des Moines and found a mechanic there who did have the code, but when the problem was explained to him he just shook his head and said, *Man, don't turn it off. Get to a dealership.* Kristen called and we talked it through, went back and forth about what to do. Of course, they should stop at a Toyota dealership we decided, but dealerships in the Midwest turned out to be generally closed on Sundays. So they decided to keep driving.

By the time they made it past Lincoln, Nebraska, it was dark and they were having second thoughts. They were still almost fourteen hours from where my parents lived in Utah—though with the way the car was acting it would be more like nineteen hours. The weather was vicious, the population density was low, and there were few cars on the road—if the car broke down, they'd be stuck out in the middle of nowhere, miles from a town, in brutally cold weather.

There was a Toyota dealership in Lincoln—I managed to get hold of someone there who was waiting for a delivery despite the dealership being closed on Sunday: he encouraged me to have Kristen bring the car in early Monday morning and he'd arrange for it to be looked at right way. So, they turned around and drove the hour back to Lincoln.

They checked into a seedy motel, slept a few hours, and then at 6:30 am Kristen drove the car over then returned to the motel to sleep. It turned out there was a crack in the radiator block that was causing the leak, and the ice building up on the front of the car had exacerbated the leak — the crack was minuscule enough that it probably wouldn't have been noticed if circumstances hadn't been just right.[3] So, when Kristen called back, she discovered that they'd removed the front end of the car. The repair was covered under warranty, but unfortunately, they didn't have the parts they needed. Where could they get parts? From Chicago, which was still reeling from the snowstorm.

There are other parts of the story — there are always other parts of any story. In this case, they involve a rental car place that my father-in-law felt was gouging him by charging him $25 a day and several cabin-fevery days in Lincoln. Kristen and I had just met a few weeks before in San Francisco a woman whose mother had gone to high school with Charlie Starkweather, but I suspected it wouldn't cheer her up if I recounted to her what I knew about the Lincoln-based murderer. The last time I'd been to Lincoln, it had been to give a reading, but the reading had been cancelled because of a blizzard — I doubted telling her this would cheer her up either.

By the time the part arrived it was Wednesday morning, the day before Thanksgiving. They packed up and drove. Kristen dropped her dad off in Salt Lake City where he could get his car and drive back up to Idaho and then drove down to Provo to meet us.

The next afternoon we ate an early Thanksgiving dinner then packed the car and drove to Las Vegas, the road snowy at first and then, almost too quickly, hot and dry. Las Vegas, as it turns out, is always Las Vegas, whether it's Thanksgiving Day or no. Early Friday morning we left again, arriving in Santa Monica later that day. A day later, I was flying back to Brown to finish teaching.

Since then, we have done our best to avoid winter. Kristen seems

---

[3] Also, the mechanic working on the car had worked for the Rhode Island dealership that had claimed nothing was wrong previously, and mistrusted this diagnosis — perhaps he felt he had something to prove.

cured of the desire to drive through snowstorms with her father, Max seems happier poolside than he ever did tromping through snow. As for me, I'm happy to be done with shoveling snow and accidentally falling; with worrying that my ear, perpetually numb from a surgery that severed the nerve, is getting frostbite without my knowing it; with Providence's winter parking bans. I do not miss winter.

But I haven't forgotten winter. I can remember going night skiing in Utah and coming home with hands and feet numb, holding them under the running lukewarm tap until they started to tingle and burn. I guess the skiing was fun, but the only thing I remember about it these days was how cold it was — so cold that even though they only charged $5 for the lift ticket almost nobody was on the slopes. I remember, as a Mormon missionary in Wisconsin, waiting with my companion for a bus in weather that was sixty degrees below zero with wind chill, and a woman stopping to beg us to accept a ride from her before we started losing extremities. *What's wrong with you?* she wanted to know. I can remember all that and more. But it's so much better to remember it from a distance, in a place where winter never comes.

When I began writing this essay, it was 112 degrees in Valencia, a heat that I would describe as unbearable. Now, a few days later, the temperature is in the 90s which feels almost temperate by comparison, particularly considering how dry it is here: if you can find some shade it feels better than 75 degrees did in humid Rhode Island. But today there are also fires raging (indeed, with climate change there seem to be fires raging all along the west coast) and the smell and haze of smoke in the air. I'm aware that people who live in climates that have winter sometimes make themselves feel better by saying things like "At least I don't have to worry about worry about wildfires and earthquakes." I don't care for this heat, and I don't care for either wildfires or earthquakes, but, I have to say, I still prefer wildfires and earthquakes to winter.

So does my son. I remember a few years ago, back before he was two, the first time we went out into weather significantly below freezing, while visiting Montpelier, Vermont. He sat at the window of our rented house staring at snowflakes and begging "Out, out." Eventually, we bundled him into his winter coat and carried him the block and a half to the edge of a forest preserve. I put him down and he touched snow and then said one of the longest sequences we had yet heard him utter: "Too cold! Too cold! Take me inside! Now!"

PLUNGE YOUR ARM IN
UP TO THE ELBOW

The ocean receded. I watch myself in the mirror. From the city head north, the directions say.

I sit on the bed in my bright green T-shirt and white shorts. My face the smooth tan of foundation. I am constructed. Everything around me is green. X-rayed baked photographed with

special equipment. Let me tell you, nobody likes me. It matches my eyes.

I watch myself in the mirror. My shirt falls squarely. Stamen flush with light. My thighs spread against the quilt. I have a body. This sets the tourist in motion.

On the day the last stone house was built I build myself in the mirror. Follow directions. I do

the cover-up. It holds me. I do the hairspray. The suck-in. I about-face. I am lonely. At one regional opening continue straight into *one day*, she says, *you'll learn to like yourself.*

PLUNGE YOUR ARM
IN UP TO THE ELBOW

At the other regional opening admire a flute of white moths.

I am still watching myself in the mirror. At its most bulbous we are at dance class. I watch myself in the mirror and feel sick. X-rayed baked photographed with special equipment.

The fluorescent light rains down hard. Turn L off the highway into the mirror. I am framed by. X-rayed, baked. At its most bulbous I am alone in the gaze. Inside the studio the sky is low

with the breath of jealous girls. I am still building what will hold me. I am that breath thickest. In the mirror I stagger after. Somewhere there's an insides. My body a flabby container. It is time

to feel something. But it cannot match my face. In the mirror I set the tourist in motion. Like a funhouse the shape wavers. See how it becomes me. I draw an X in the steam of breath on the

mirror. It is time to close the gateway of the ribs or spill out. It's my turn to cross the floor.

We put water balloons down our bathing suit tops that summer and posed for pics. After driving 92.3 mi all I see is her beauty. As one blunt thing I have no body. I must separate into parts.

TO BE OR *LIKE* NOT TO BE

The ocean receded. I sit on the bleachers in my cotton gym shorts.
Over the blunt ends of my knees I watch her fight back. Rites of
passage. She throws the basketball *like* right in Natalie's

face

her black hair like two curtains ripped open. Black widow's peak,
her mouth ringed orange like fun. The spit of cover-up parts her
black hair. What surprise lights up her wicked white girl face.

What wicked white girl face of my dreams. The gymnasium floor
shrieks. I watch her *like* claw out. Out out. Girl pieces whir. Her
fingers in motion. Aware the pronoun's confusing. It's true

they pull hair. I am not *like* a fighter but you have to kill the pretty
girl. Middle school queen. You have to dig in with your body. I
watch. See my fingers curl. I watch them get physical.

Right through the make-up. Right out our wicked white scene.
Heat bloods to the surface and mingles. Another *like* sistering.
Silver hoops hook and tear. What I wouldn't give to dig in.

See the red smear pop on the lacquered floor. Where the sun hits
it's blinding. I squint over the blunt end of my knees. All I want
is a body. To rip into. Not my own. Not my own legs.

TO BE OR *LIKE* NOT TO BE

The ocean receded. I puff around the oval track. Gravel nips my shins. *Say your name and a verb that begins with the same letter. Do the motion.* I puff around the oval track. I grasp the stick in

one hand. *J is for —* *J is for —* I watch her silver hoop earrings her bright blond hair. See me follow. Her blond hair bounce, tail of her white polo fluttering. See me follow. My breath *like*

burns. We each see the ball, grasp our stick hooked and handled. See her sprint down the field. Her lips curl back see two eye teeth even whiter than pearl. See her verb things. *S is for sinuous*

S is for supple S is for sex

-y. She holds the field hockey stick across her hips in two fists. *Miss Piggy Miss Piggy* she sings. The stick hooked and handled. *J is for —* She pugs her nose with one finger and laughs. See

my own fingers curl.

PLUNGE YOUR ARM
IN UP TO THE ELBOW

I watch the pretty girls roll up their tights. Leg by leg. I don't even want to visit my body. I don't want the ground. I scratch my white thigh. I must have something. I pull up my hem. Feet slap

the blond boards. I tug and I tug and I tug. This sets the tourist in motion.

How to posture elsewhere. Map out the roads to her cave. To make her cloud animals dance at a look. I hold the red-brown smears to my nose and inhale. It is not the same as your blood. Here

is where the forest will part. I am hoarding secrets off the map. To make her lakes gleam blue. To gleam blue in reflection. No one would step off the path if there's path. Tell me your lies.

I peer out between the leaves of my anger. Lonely leaves. They match my green eyes. The girls are dancing the path their pale pink tights trace a longing. A flutter like wings in the dust. If you

look in my eyes you can see the reflection. This sets the tourist in motion.

That summer a boy puts his hands down my pants. It hurt. Over and over it hurt. My toes bloody from dancing. I tug and I tug and I tug. The truth is I like a little pain. That summer I buy my

first skirt.

RABBIT BOT

うさぎ島の写真BOT

no predators on Rabbit Isle memory's a poison gas over it

war in this place never gave it a name kept it hidden

maybe I'll have that agency someday erase an island you know

read they might've come from few as eight rabbits

eat what they're fed & flourish pushed leafy greens from hand but go hungry unphotographed in the cold

hunger born when men invented comfort light needing dark like I need my list of complications

in this story I'm a savior but I don't know yet if I'm the kind meant to sacrifice

for those raised on nothing but dependence all domestic hang my flag on the wall near the cross

stitched quilt hang it near the hole where wind creeps in

it's when they tell me it's time to mend but I don't partake

I stay up all night put off warmth crumple my paper shriek something

remember this when I've got my rabbits around me coat
made of silver & glass my steady hand

understand being nowhere make do with what we have I too
was alone in the dark

womb make do with what we have why I wrote you that letter

put in a bottle sealed up threw out in the ocean not that
it'd find you but make its own way

before summer feeling new love a day's responsibility ice sheet
bills piled anything else comes along to ruin a plan

before my rabbits learn ease was always an enemy time
comes for us all the same

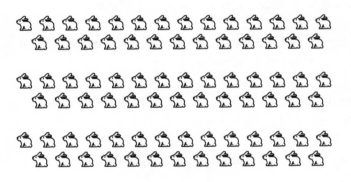

AGING AND CINICAL [SIC]

not surprising
that
             im
aging.
im
poorly.
B's relatives
             know.
             (i   owe
      pa   a
  note.)   i   act
strong.   i   act
on the
       logic   that
            art
  means
            omen.   f---
Gene/Environment!
              The
            Heart
            weighs
            three
dimes'   weight,
    Still
            is
            strong.

(Source for this erasure: Haller S, et al. "Cerebral Microbleeds: Imaging and Clinical Significance." *Radiology* 287(1):16, 2018.)

DEEP MEN

deep

men

carry

the risk of

setting

a   lo / bar.

deep   m-

en   are strong

with burden of white

intensities.

pathologic,

clearly high.

almost in-

variably

sensitive,

patient

men   who

will not   play,

certainly supportive in the appropriate

setting.

MR.

Comb,   we can

summarize: between the

decline

and

further decline,

the average

did not   control

me.

might i
suggest i
decline
to be

treat-
ed
as
hemorrhage?
i   posit   complication.
                            agnostic, i
search
his
valence;
no   true
fact

                        i   find.

(Source for this erasure: Haller S, et al. "Cerebral Microbleeds: Imaging and Clinical Significance." *Radiology* 287(1):16, 2018.)

RIDE OR DIE

Of course it is, like I said. Iced tea. You're going to want to pace yourself. My thinking was we would start on the Mad Dog after the swim. One hour give or take. Hour five. Give or take. Not much wave action this morning, and she's feeling strong, so let's say take. Managed to get down two tablespoons of whey back at the microtel. Four lucky spoonfuls of creamed wheat. Managed to save all her jitter-shits for this here fleet of Portajohns. Which — if you were thinking they were here for the spectators, you have another thing —. Just see if there's even an inch of toilet paper, for instance, in any one. You've got to figure, upwards of three thousand athletes and every one of them ate ten times their body weight in grams of carbohydrate exactly twenty-four hours ago. I wouldn't worry. I'm not worried. Once the sun's up, you're going to be sweating faster than you can drink. You're going to be, trust me, diving for the cooler. And that's when we start on the six-pack, was my thinking.

NEXRAD's showing spotty clouds over the foothills, wind at 2.4 m/s, 280 degrees west-northwest. Negligible headwind. Nothing major in terms of crosswinds, yaw. What we're looking at is general cloud cover across the valley right around the middle of leg two. That's when Gwenn is remembering the run ahead, consciously allowing herself to fall back through the chase pack. Gwenn races smart now she has a coach. For a lot of these athletes, their weakness is thinking the bike is their strength.

Cloud cover is great. Generally great and specifically great as far as race photos go. Gwenn is top five in her age bracket in the water. Top thirty on the bike. The run is a toss —. I mean a crapshoot. As far as smiles go, I don't need to tell you where our girl ranks. Photographers have actually been known to stake her out. This year, if nothing else, she's going to make the highlight reel. Cross the finish line with a smile on. That's the mission. No matter the slosh, the bonk, the bloat, the chafe. Make it look fun. Be one of those women who make it look fun.

Sam Swift of MyTriJourney.com.

Amy D of the six distinct deep-scored thigh muscles, of the practically concave chest, of the effectively concave tum. Amy D of the ten official 'm-dot' tattoos, one for every time she's 'gone to the big island.'

That one who claims she eats only avocados.

Quadzilla.

Sponsorship would change things for her. For us. She could use a new helmet, wetsuit. She could use a smart trainer. Everyone who is anyone is training to a meter these days. Gone is the era of 'follow your heart.'

Not that she's asking me, or even going to. But I know. I know she could use a bike. No matter how many times I have said, 'It's the biker not the bike,' the fact is: it is the bike. That road bike was fine when she was doing sprint tris, halfs. She's beyond that now. She doesn't wear underwear under her race bib anymore. She doesn't even have nails on half her toes.

But she can't keep letting me buy all her gear, is the thing. When it was canoeing, it was different, because that was an activity we both enjoyed. The way Gwenn sees it, ninety percent of the purpose of becoming an Ironman — again — and again, every month of the summer — is about accruing self-worth. And you can't very well do that, I mean Gwenn can't very well do that, I mean Gwenn can't very well allow herself to do that, that is, to continue doing that, on someone else's dime.

Give or take six fifty. Six hundred and fifty. Dollars. Per race. Give or take.

So she's holding out for a sponsor. Someone official, someone not-me.

To give you an idea: more than her engagement ring, the bike.

25

And that is — we're talking low-mid-grade. Draggy spokes. We're not talking fully electric drivetrain. We're not talking toroidal carb-alloy rims. We're not talking aerobottles or rear discs or Accelerade over there and Mr. EnDura-whatever trying to draft on his paceline.

Her paceline. Oh.

So that makes sixteen.

Women.

Sixteen. One-six.

That is sort of what I do, professionally. Counting. It is my principle occupational function. I know, the title is misleading. What can I say? The hype is misleading. The degree and career path and academic counsel are misleading. The R and the D are misleading. My greatest discovery of the past year — of the past five maybe — was that a bound journal volume placed just-so on a keyboard can effectively simulate productivity. Mine is what you call high-workload low-taskload work. I am the sort of engineer whose job consists of passively monitoring a complex system in anticipation of a problem. I exist in a state of vigilance and vague anxiety that is equal parts misery and fatigue.

You have to figure that sixteen includes all twelve of the elites, and those last two at least were out of her age range. I do mean older. A good rule of thumb is you take the age you're thinking and you add ten. One way the Tough gets going when the going gets tough is she calls up and holds in her mind images of sixty-year-old, seventy-year-old athletes who do not look a day over forty-five. One way the Tough gets to sleep at night is scrolling, scrolling through Instagram.

Luca thinks Gwenn would look good in Soy Joy pink — something modern, like Oatmega teal. But the dream sponsor, the sponsor of her dreams, is Farina. Race day fuel par excellence. Farina, still Farina, always Farina. These days she doctors it with golden honey and forty-five milligrams of C-PRO Performance Electrolyte Powder. Which is another word for sodium, which is another word for — . It is blue, and I cannot say why it is blue, and it goes for sixty dollars a pound, and unless you make the mistake of buying it in lemon-lime, it does not have a smell.

She will not put her lucky spoon in until the gruel is sweaty and membranous. Until it is uniform in tinge, the color of denim lint. Only when her mealmeal gets like half-set epoxy will she dig in, eat until her nerves cannot be distinguished from nausea from heartburn from indigestion from upset stomach—. I mean, I get it. I grew up on that stuff too. Not Farina. I mean the idea that persisting in an unpleasant activity is the key to success. It's an insidious yet seductive perversion of logic. It is probably mostly-accurate to say that nothing great gets done without considerable hard work. Or whatever your preferred formulation. 'Gotta bleed to succeed.' 'If it were easy…' etc. I have no beef with that. But reversing your premises there gets you something tantamount to, well, to magical thinking. A delayed gratification fetish.

But this is neither the time nor the place—. When thousands of athletes from dozens of countries are here converting their forty weeks (or four (or forty) years) of ten-hours-per-week weeks of dedication and sacrifice and fortitude-in-the-face-of—and, in some cases, reckless spousal expenditure—into something like total spiritual consummation. If you have not witnessed a finish line, then I really can't explain.

I'm telling you, this music even starts to make sense.

I was always more of a Frosted Flake myself. Honestly I thought Farina was some sort of tooth-whitening solution. Because that kid. From the box? I used to tell Gwenn she looked just like him. And she really does. Up at Breck, when she takes her helmet off? Like health itself.

Speaking of.

That one. That one is her. I know by her dance. I know that's her because the first thing she does when she hits land is bang on her head like that. She's been a swimmer since she was what, and she still can't stand the feel of water in her ears. Or is it the sound?

It's like how, no matter how many trainer-hours Gwenn logs

with no matter how many trainers at no matter how many gyms, and no matter how many configurations of midsole cushions and medial posts and heel counter inserts and stability cradles and AI socks, she still over-pronates like a goose. Or like how no matter how many times she tells herself she loves to run — .

Exactly. If she has to tell herself.

One hour by my watch. That's just off her PR. By off I mean under. So that's pretty good, so I'm going to give her the thumbs up. She can be happy with that. I'm going to give her the thumbs, and then I'm going to swing the shit out of this thing, and then we are going to run to the other side of the T1 tent, where they get them skinned like seals and slapped all over with SPF lube in six minutes or less. And then I'm going to give her the thumbs and crank this thing some more.

Please. I'm an engineer. Obviously I was not going to settle for a finger whistle, pennies in a milk jug. Fucking bambam sticks.

It was nothing at all to throw together. You just need a knife and an awl, a ruler, a drill, a 13/32-inch and a 25/64-inch drill bit, scrap wood and wood shards and three wooden blocks, dowels, grippy tape, craft glue, and sandpaper, and a vise. And paint. Purple if you want to make her happy, if you really want to make her happy.

Her career was not, not making her happy. Showed zero signs of progressing in the direction of doing so. Turns out, everyone with Gwenn's background was banking on the same vague something. Environmental Consulting. The number of geology grads coming out of top tier universities with every intention of going to war for sustainability was not, frankly, *sustainable*. When we moved here, we found out that her degree could get her a job in exactly one of two fields: 1) mining, 2) surveying. It could get her a job any day, anywhere in the country, in oil and gas.

I'm sure you have not forgotten our first summer here. Gwenn's time in Aggregates? Ten hour days of concrete testing.

Tens of hours of minutes of seconds that passed at the pace of concrete. It simply wasn't her idea of a life.

Not that a job has to make you happy. Not that you should expect it to. A job should make you money; that is what you should expect a job to do. But I don't want to argue. We all have our own definition of tenable minimums. We're all operating, to some extent, on spec.

See but as long as she's smiling, you can tell it's her, can't you?

You think it's hard now, wait till they are helmeted. Wait till they are aeroposed. Wait till they are 50 mph projectiles. Wait until ten hours from now, when everything is sweated flat, everyone is slack-jawed and staggering, vibrantly chapped and chafed. A mob of animatrons flooding the canal path. Grim. Jerky. Genderless adrenaline puppets.

I hope you will stay. It's something like you don't get to see outside of movies. And I have a whole nother gallon of that tea at my cache. 800 yards from the shuttle stop, 400 yards from the Finish, on ice, in a tree.

My outpost is at the bottom of the course's steepest hill, so that every time Gwenn passes, she will see me (or us) and feel my (or our) love, and she won't even think about taking it at a walk. Even if she maybe *should* take it at a walk. Even if sixty percent of age-groupers and forty percent of age-groupers in her age-group take it, at least one time through, at something between a shuffle and a stagger. Even if it puts her nearer her max VO2 than she ought to be at at any point before the homestretch. Because Gwenn has a tendency to fixate on failure and to simultaneously fail to distinguish between minor failures and major ones. To stop, to slow, to Gwenn, is to quit. But you know this: Gwenn's mind is a slippery slope. Gwenn's mind is the descent off Hawi, at Kona, where world-class cyclists have been known to spin out. We've known this all along. It's one of the reasons this sport is so great for her, has been so critical, in terms of providing a natural, built-in, incremental reward system. A mock battle to sate her warrior brain.

It helps to know her bike is bluish, her cleats are purple, sneakers purple and green. She wears a wristwatch, purple; and her bib is black with purple. And it helps to know the number on it, which is 616, because that's her favorite, because it's our anniversary, and you bet we were first in line when early registration opened, when she smuggled me into and before I got booted from Athlete Village, after last year's post-race festivities.

Festivities. Libations. Keynotes. Yes. The finish line is not the end. Medals. Ribbons. Your full money's-worth. Brought to you by Cozmic Pizza. Brought to you by Rodie's Rolfery.

A shuttle departs every ten minutes from the lot behind the taco truck and the drivers do not care if or what you drink aboard. You can shuttle to the Finish or you can shuttle to the Finish and from there walk to the city's finest rooftop margarita bar. You can order one margarita dry and one margarita skinny and you can drink them slow and still have time to arrive at the Finish before Gwenn does. What you cannot do is you cannot drive yourself out of here, in the case that you did want to. Not until after the Cut-off: ten hours and twenty minutes from the moment the last aquatic thrasher waddles ashore. You'll know because all those jet skis and dinghies and paddleboards — and sometimes some waterfowl, too — will close in around the individual, the straggler, and cheer him in, or haul him in, as the case may be. From this distance, it may look, now and then, like a public execution by drowning.

Usually it is a him. Men are more likely to believe, in the absence of any relevant indication, that there is something — some *thing* inside them — that will spring to heroic action when certain preconditions are met. They are willing to wager a good deal in pride and registration fees for a chance at such an encounter.

Usually it's an old-ass man with a heart condition, arthritis, and scuba goggles.

I hope you will stay. But I understand if you can't, or won't. I understand if there is somewhere you have to be, or something you feel you should do, or see, or eat, or drink, or buy, or otherwise experience, beyond these barricades and the giant inflatable sports drink totems. I could understand if you wanted to take refuge from the noisemaking or the Ironband hype set or the sun. Because it's only going to get hotter, and Billy Beats of KBCO-Boulder is only going to get hoarser, and down on the creek path it is going to get frankly buggy.

Three and change for the first circuit; three point five for the second.

We could — I don't know. Someone here has to have a hacky sack.

Where we'll set up, if you stay, is right around a bend, for that extra jolt of surprise. We'll be ready when she comes, because it's the least we can do. It is literally the least a person can do. Rare and beautiful are the occasions in this life when you can do so much by just remaining. Existing. Attending.

Or I don't know. Beautiful at least.

She'll pass us three times on foot. She'll pretend to be surprised the second and the third time. She'll be pretending the first time too. Don't think for a second that my location was not a part of Gwenn's race-day plan. She has placed me at the post-underpass, pre-hill bend the way she has placed, at the mile forty-seven special aid station, glucose shots and contact lenses, a spare bike tube, and notes of encouragement from the fans and fam.

In the interim we can vote on our favorite grimace or rictus or mode of capitulation. Guarantee we see at least one Total Buckle. You ever seen those fainting goats? Some sorry pro-tender will sit down right there in the center of the path, like the oncoming hill straight up sucker punched em.

There is also always the possibility of a trampling.

What we have here in these zip-top baggies is seventy percent water, thirty percent pureed organic citrus. When she passes, we will stand prepared to, if she gives the signal, punch a suck-hole and trot alongside her for a pace so that she can take a drink without losing stride. A lightning round of Slap-the-bag.

Her hydration plan has been the work of several months. She is better than anyone I know at recording intricate variations on a spreadsheet and putting those data to work. I knew this about her before I knew just about anything else. Before I knew, I think, that I loved her.

We met in a fluid dynamics lab she claimed to be struggling with. I offered to help because I thought I was doing OK and I thought she was, well —. You know.

She ended up tutoring me and half the class.

She has worked out how many tabs of salt she is going to need on the run if the thermometer on her wristwatch gets above 80 by the time she hits T2. We know now — in fact we have known since that starting gun went off at 6:53 a.m. — in fact we have known since last month — that in the next four to seven minutes, she'll be cresting that hill. We know that at 7:10 p.m., she will be more or less puddled under a tree by the Library. Draped in one of those gaudy Mylar capes like a queen.

And then she will have her Snickers bar.

What she'll do is she will hold onto it for awhile. Until she can feel it's the appropriate temperature. The approximate temperature of her skin. Because there is nothing like a Snickers bar at a moment like this and so there is also nothing like the anticipation of a Snickers bar at a moment like this. If you plan it out right, you can sort of always live in some shade of this, of coming incrementally closer to something you not only want but also feel you deserve.

I should warn you: she may or may not even eat the candy bar, as we sit there. By we, I mean, you, me, and all of the tri friends you will have the opportunity to meet today, if you stay. It turns out, it's as easy to make friends at a tri as it is to make friends at a bar. And it's a lot like making friends at a bar, too. No one expects you to remember their name or bothers remembering yours, and they even refer to their post-exerted state as 'trashed.' It's also about as difficult to get rid of tri friends as it is to get rid of bar friends, or to get rid of, say, wet trash. They are heavier than they seem they should be, and often they are fit to —. Well. Surely she has mentioned the issue with vomiting? How it happens? At the races? A lot?

She tells everyone, so I assumed.

She will eat her Snickers bar only when she has the sense that she's fully in control of her fluid's dynamics. You should not be offended if she doesn't want to talk, or wants to talk only about how she needs to pee and is afraid to pee.

I am sure if she has told you about the vomiting then she has also told you about the pissing blood?

I had thought maybe we had reached the end of something the day the soreness in her nethers turned out to be actual sores. She has never been one to refrain from picking at scabs, if you can imagine. I felt like, Who is this hulking primate and what has become of my pretty wife? If I didn't want to look at her inguinal scabs, she would leave them places, line them up on the booze unit or the breakfast nook for me to see when I wasn't at work.

'Morning Fuel Nook' — sorry. We no longer use words like breakfast, lunch, and dinner. They are charged. We no longer use or have use for the word 'brunch' because she eats with such frequency that the idea of ever collapsing two mealmeals into one is absurd. It goes without saying that when I make a cocktail she doesn't partake. Gwenn has important nutritional needs and no time for empty calories. And Gwenn has a fearsome love of Snickers bars. I mean that in a literal sense. She is afraid of her love of Snickers bars. So much so that she only feels they are permitted on occasions such as this. On occasions of sustained high-energy expenditure lasting thirteen hours. Sorry, just under thirteen hours. If she breaks thirteen as a woman of thirty-four who has competed in fewer than four prior Ironmans, she will set a record.

Yes, this is a thing people keep track of.

Everyone thinks they are a bit much sometimes. Women especially. That's my experience. I bet you come with all kinds of disclaimers yourself. That's what I told Gwenn when we first got hooked up. That, not to invalidate all of her concerns, but I wasn't scared of whatever amount of crazy she thought she was bringing to the table. This was someone who, let me remind you, essentially co-taught grad FLD lab. So it was hard to imagine that she would get it in her head that, for instance, the most important thing in life was to lose three pounds. Or that this was someone who would just evaporate into a Facebook feed. Or that she could spend a week thinking only about the way a certain section of her abdomen looked when she leaned forward five degrees at the countertop, such as when she was preparing us meals.

She stopped preparing us meals when the training started, because it turns out that any sort of meal you can cook doesn't really address the high-intensity needs of the high-intensity athlete. After a while, it was not only was she getting the right nutrients and minerals at the right time but was she properly absorbing them, was she properly metabolizing them.

What she eats for fuel — I should say, what she fuels with (eat being another of those words) — comes in small metallic pouches and takes the form of either powder or goo or jellied cubes. She is almost always wearing some form of fuel or hydration or mineral replenishment or some combination thereof within her garments, stuffed up inside her sports bra. Otherwise she keeps them in the drawer with the dog treats.

The dog thing was short-lived. We went through several, of various sizes and breeds, from the pound of course, and couldn't find a single one that wasn't driven up the walls by Gwenn's trainer. Her trainer is the 'ultra quiet' magnetic resistance snap-mount kind, 'no louder' — per Sam Swift's *Sam Swift Reviews* review — 'than a large-load SpeedQueen set to spin' (for four hours a day three days a week).

The trainer was non-negotiable. First off because training for a June race means starting in December; and second off, because the Springs have near-zero elevation gain and altogether too many traffic lights, Gwenn says. With the trainer, she can envision herself back here, where she wishes we still lived.

Luca's been a major consolation as far as the Springs are concerned. Had my office not moved us out to Englewood, he never would have found her lap swimming at the neighborhood Y.

That's how he puts it. 'Found.'

That's how she puts it, too.

Everyone wants to feel found, I think. Everyone wants to feel saved and set on a path that leads to a journey that makes them a hero. It's something that every person has a right to experience in this life. Why would I want to deny her that?

You think my job makes me happy? That I love research? You know what I research? I research whose ass I get to kiss next. I research how to explain rapid prototyping via additive manufacturing to bored-ass board members, how to communicate selective laser sintering in basically charades. I basically perform charades and hope that whichever shareholder holds the most shares has had a decent lunch. But those are the fun days! When I'm not doing that, I am at my desk, carrying out selective operations to reach certain limited conclusions the validity of which is subject to verification by an anonymous third-party researcher or research group or for all the fuck I know computer algorithm. My specialty is solving the same problem again and again and when they run into the same problem I have solved before, they come to me with the problem because they are aware that I am 'good at' fixing it. And no I am not going to put it in concrete terms for you, sorry, because it is the weekend and *the weekend is for living*.

They are not aware, at work, that I no longer spend my weekends on the water. I no longer spend the weekends paddling or portaging or fishing or blazing trail, as all the photos on my desk suggest, as my auto-renewing subscription to *BACKPACKER* suggests, as my ninety-five percent lightweight nylon five percent spandex wardrobe suggests. They are not aware that most weekends I am here, on the sidelines, with my cooler and baggies, my homemade rattle. My hilarious tee-shirt, my any number of hilarious tee-shirts.

I – am – Iron – Lump!

It's a big fat fucking joke what a big fat fucking joke I am.

Meanwhile Gwenn's got her Quadzilla, her Amy D, her Sam Swift. These titans of the tri that sort of radiate success. Bionic women she would like so much to be. Who, when they say things like, 'You should not compare yourself to others,' it sounds like the most obvious thing in the world. And when Gwenn says it? When Gwenn says it, it sounds shrill, like a mantra, like a plea. Like something that holds up a great deal else.

Because all we do is compare. All we ever do. Like here I am, forty pounds overweight, and wondering what my wife must think of me. Right? Because if she can't bear to look at herself in those photos from graduation, where she had, I don't know, gone a little soft at the obliques? Then what does she think when she looks at me?

Of course she is not going to leave me. Gwenn is never going to leave me. Our love is –. Our love is one hundred percent the bedrock and foundation of her existence.

I am her without-which nothing.

I can't begrudge Gwenn for becoming unrecognizable, for becoming someone entirely other from the cute blonde on the mantle. Because I am nothing like the man who made forever promises before an audience of friends and family and you. And yes, we keep our wedding album on the mantle, and yes, I think that wedding albums were invented to invite the first moments of conflict and tension in to a new marriage. I think wedding albums were conceived to introduce an end right from the start. What happens is that one of you wants the thing to be out, to be open, wants to share it with every single person who enters the house, and at the same time wants a second copy, a private copy, that is preserved and untouched and in some sort of lightbox in the master suite. And that person is probably also the one who wants to make a sort of love-shrine in the living room with all the valentines that you have ever exchanged; and that person is also the sort to clip on the fridge mundane notes in which you signed off with cute, very personal diminutives. Even the ones from her race stash, yellow and totally illegible from sweat and friction.

Some people burn out. It usually happens around year three. And other people — . Well. Have you ever heard of the Deca Ironman?

Deca. From the Greek, *deka*. Meaning ten?

Luca's previous protégé went all the way to the world championship just to go over her handlebars on a stretch ride. Acromioclavicular joint separation thirty-some hours to Send-off. One arm hanging five inches below the shoulder, like a stuffed toy you shouldn't have put in the wash. Of course she raced. Did the whole thing in a sling: talk about a white-knuckle ride.

Others, pre-Gwenn, 'ended up with kids.' Which isn't to say kids are always or necessarily the end of things as far as competition is concerned. One of his Ironmoms, for instance — a Category 3/Cat 2-hopeful cyclocrosser — used to do all her training jogs around the block when her son was in diapers. Water bottle in one hand, baby monitor in the other.

True, eventually, she had seen her neighbor's hedges one time too many, and against the advice of her husband and their pediatrician, and all husbands and pediatricians everywhere, took her baby out for ten miles of hard fartleks in a baby bjorn. I think she got arrested around mile two.

People ask you about it. It's inevitable, once you've been in it awhile: 'Have you ever thought about — *Kona*?'

Gwenn says 'No,' but I don't know. She doesn't say it the same way anymore.

It's not like I think she'll never work. It's just that she can't do anything that feels like or looks like work right now. Because to do so would be to admit that she has wasted years of her life and so many thousands of dollars. By the time eight years have gone by, the eight years she spent acquiring her expertise won't trouble her quite so much anymore. That's what I think. Maybe she'll get another degree. Maybe she'll formulate her own line of high-performance goo.

I don't fault her for pursuing what makes her happy. Of course, I don't. If there were anything in the world that I found that gave me a joy and sense of fulfillment that even approached the joy and sense of fulfillment this sport brings her, I would want to orient myself towards and around that, at any cost.

I should not say cost. It's not about the money. It's really not. It's not about race registration and fuel and Luca and PT and exotic locations. I could fly us both to the Big Island of Hawai'i for five days with the money I make in a week. I could fill a whole room, a whole floor, of our house with framed photo finishes.

So it's not that. It's about how I don't know what comes next. What happens when she finishes this race? What happens when she crosses that finish line today or next year or the year after, in Coeur d'Alene, in Queensland, in Cannes or — who knows — even Kona? What happens when she wants more? What is there, what more?

Listen, I used to use recreational chemicals, let's call them. I was not an addict. I don't know if you can even be addicted to volatile organic solvents. But something I know is that you can't sniff glue forever. What I'm saying is you don't just get to feel as good as Gwenn feels when she finishes the race. You don't just get to have that joy and keep it. And I'm scared. I am scared about what is going to happen, next week, or next year, when it happens, when it's not enough, what I am supposed to do.

I brought up the dog, again, a few months back. I didn't even mean to. It's just that I never imagined myself 35 and with no dog around. And with that sizeable (and I am being modest) house we have out there. And with all that yard. All I said was that dogs are good for follows and follows are good for sponsorship prospects, but Gwenn just looked at me. Neither of us has time to walk a dog. I knew this. She knew I knew this. Walking a dog does not figure into Gwenn's weekly training goals (WTG), nor does it figure into her MTG or her YTG or LTG, all of which Luca has printed in tabular format on *YOU ARE IRONMAN* magnets, decals, binders, swim caps, and chamoix, such that all Gwenn had to do that day was sigh and roll her eyes in just about any direction in our modestly-enormous home for me to catch her drift, recognize that I was being unfair, the opposite of a noodlemuffin. The opposite of a sugarbooger.

When she finally said something, the argument was so over it came out all sage and axiomatic. I think what she said — inverted over one of her giant foam rollers on the family room floor — was: 'Dogs introduce an element of unpredictability not accounted for or reflected in my lifetime training goals.'

You know how Gwenn is about control. So you of all people can appreciate how great it is that she's learning to shift that in a positive direction. How she has this outlet, these role models, this support. How she has this newfound respect for her body as machine. How she doesn't have an unhealthy obsession, anymore, with food.

It's really great. And it's great that you are here. All that way and at no small expense for a weekend trip, when I understand that they are still paying you in basically promissory notes? So that's, well. That's just so kind of you. It's really just huge.

And I hope you will stay. But I understand if you can't. I understand if you can't, or won't, or if there is somewhere else you have to go. I understand if there is something else you feel you need to do, or see, or something else, somewhere else, you can sit and sneer at. Something not-this. Something not-us. Because you realize, don't you, what a surprise it must be? To see you. You and your shoulders. Not the nice kind of surprise, like the

Snickers bar in the cooler, which we only pretend is a surprise when there are friends and supporters around. No. The bad kind of surprise, where she is going to think that she has been mistaken, that shoulders like that were something that she might have, at some point in her life, been moving towards. That she has fallen now, off course.

You could at least have sleeves on.

Let me tell you something about trajectories. I had believed — I had been *led* to believe — that I would eventually come to a place where what mattered to me in my life was my work. Still sometimes I wish that were the case. But what happens is you reach the place where the momentum of your education and innate abilities was going to end up carrying you all along. And then you are just there, and wondering, 'Is this all there is?'

I had thought I might engineer a solution that would benefit many. Well it turns out, all I've figured out is how to help one. One person. My wife. I no longer believe there is anything I am capable of doing that would outweigh that in terms of importance.

Is this all there is?

Yes. Yes, and so what?

Yes, I have wanted to eat the goddamned Snickers bar. Yes, waiting on the sidelines for her to finish the race, or after, I have wanted to rip it out of her hands. But that's because —. That's what you don't understand. This is the difficult thing. This is the thing which not anyone can do. This is the thing where, you can only hope at the end of it, you come out smiling.

Now, if you wouldn't mind standing back a ways? My wife needs the noise, and I don't want to clock you with this thing.

DEWEY SQUARE SEQUENCE

1. Mid-March

It's seven pm & atlantic
avenue at summer street
is streaked with
red; Rose-

Kennedy's Greenway
in snow:
dulcet beauty
singing the stricture

of dirt,
of ice scored
in grimy heaps
beneath drowsy boughs

I drift across evening
(as Spring hymns
through every stone)
cold & bright!

2. Symphony at Summer Street

car metal orchestra
at   dusk;
cement choir humming
at first light;

idle engines thrumming
through rests
stoplights conduct,
switch

bloom & all brake
into song! what bid
the city speak? lilt
at such a turn of light

at such a precise
moment as this?
imagine: a musing heart,
an ineffable composition

3. Myth

When upon
a scream of tooth-point stars
Os cast away
      a wish —

at once forgot
raw throated suns! his cosmos:
cacophonic thrift —

his wish begot, the stars
are hush: tongues of seed

thick with thrush: what shined
turned: pallid, husk: Os unearthed

silence: light: wrought out the dusk . . .

4. Mural
after Shinique Smith & The Pandolfo Brothers

a rose revolves apart from a
jaw   of black space   petal
and sapphire bloom bend
along   a   coal   moon
diametric — Os became home
hunched over Dewey Square
seven   stories   tall
massive yellow face: a
storybook moon; galactic
two-piece checkered blue and
terraform   green;   sports
coat-headscarf dyed Mars
paint — fifth dimension style —
sung tight to the stonewall.

5. Another Way to Tell a Truth

Atlantic Ave: petal-red palms above evening traffic: sedans
& towncars sighing to rest
Os hums: hymns of self: (starfled
silence): my mouth:

Sudden cityscape harping stellate gardens: quiet comets
of light between
two throats breathing radiant
figures to life:

I watch: They dance(mute on stone): a timeless jig: I watch
They drift
flare: flicker: evanesce . . .
away:

I wonder: *what is left, after all?*: (& Spring splits too) lips:
a field of questions: *what else
to become? ineffable?*: pull a star out my teeth
instead: (*make a wish*): & I drop it.

GUESSING GAME

after Claudia Rankine

There was a time when me and whitefolk played this game
but pretended not to—

Guess Which Blackboy I Am

—split over grape-flavored blunts, a backhanded
joke aimed to coax the wound out the backwood

The Contusion, A Token's Token

to start the game. We dapped up.
You called me the wrong name:

	Nathaniel,	*right? I remember*		*the flat top cut.*
Or	*Aaron! What's good*	*nigga?*		
Or	we didn't	dap up, but	you	stranger

White-Noise In The House Of Blues

snatched	static	out	my hair.	*Hi, my name is*
	Property,	*Your Property.*		—you win.
Check the fine print:	*All*	*Rights Are*		*Void.*

Gin me to cotton-white smoke and watch
my bones brim inside
                              out; exhausted and beside myself
we waxed fatalic, mused about dissociation:

if   a nigga is   a nigga for   "acting niggerish"
rockin hoodies   saggin pants or "being" "too loud"
                         &
if   'my nigga' is   my homie is   my brother is
my best friend is

                         a whiteboy . . .

in what context do I help reforge the word
          in his mouth? Hone it sharp enough to carve
friendship in my skin with our history?

The day I understood . . .

          I was hanging in his basement—

I was wading through   a history of whetstones   and
     absently, shut off the light.
He called after me,   at the door: *Come on, nigga . . .*
     nigga!

I think I felt most Black confined to the dark static
          of that hallway, white-noise resonant enough to put me
     in check.

Or was it context?

          Why it felt like he meant to call me my name?

I found the light   right outside
          and went home.

VENDING MACHINE JUNKIE

found perfect places for my spaces here.

the Internet is not my friend

wasting
time
for
a dollar
twenty-five.

politely stated.

sonars
the silence

deadening
the beauty
the sparkles

subterranean caves
cuevas

sunken. floating. spinning.

overrated
under. Call importance

lost litter box

tacked swan wings.
flies swarming with bodies

scraping. merry daggers listening
inside nature. screens bacterium

Hostage. Encrypted. Walls full of whalers. Wildlife Sparks. Sparks full of stars. Contraband. Splendor. Boxes full of open fields. Fossilized boxes. Redwoods full of blooming boxes. In browns, yellows, tanned tape buoyant. Labeled. Rows. Boxes full of universe teeth.

AFTER PAPA MURIÓ,
AFTER MY FATHER DIED

I did *nada*
Nothing

his aftershave sprinkler
old spice drip

hospice

everyone prayed chanted
I the poet said nothing, nada.

eulogy etched in dots on my bleached skin

tiny teeth grazed my eyes

motionless subway to Richmond
Antioch Yellow

We call Freeways 836 East

I 95 takes you all the way to New York
return for a partial refund after 30 days

sticker removed from the glitter tulle pink salamanders

salmonella greeting every blade
palmettos parting gifts

iguanas turquoise blue
on my meshed doorstep.

Los fantasmas the ghosts waited under the white tent
Steaming gravel bought at the 99-cent store

Our skin blushed with 8st homedepot terra cotta pots in
      goldengrub shade

Open early Christmas Box untaped november
Octogenarian Cuban boned body
Exquisite tongue of the forked skillet
Weighing
Down my birth.
In *Agua de Violetas*

GROCERY STORE ARMAGEDDON

All the college-aged women who lived at the Haste Street apartments were smart enough for celibacy but not intellectual enough to be able to rationalize this omission with something convincing and filling, like a feminist slant involving our bodies, our selves, or a planned moratorium on all things corporeal for the sake of an immaculate academic record unstained with pills and alternate plans. Instead, we spent our unburdened evenings talking metaphorically about our organs.

"But does he speak to your heart?" someone would invariably say, every time one of us expressed some moot interest in a graduate student instructor, or older gentleman at church who worked at Kaiser and was a homeowner, albeit in the sketchy side of town.

"Your heart is like a cookie," I offered once.

"Go on, tell them," said Esther, who used to be beautiful before she got bottom-heavy.

"And every time you like someone, you give a little bite of your cookie away," I said to a rapt audience of blank faces and tidy vaginas.

"Then what?" said Sooyeon, who baked and watched basketball, a double entendre.

"Then when you get married, you'll have nothing left to give to your husband — just crumbs," I said.

Everyone nodded, chewing more slowly on Esther's chicken katsu, as if suspicious of a hidden bone or tendon beneath all that breading. Lesser women than us saved just their bodies; we were saving our hearts. We treated crushes and tingly sensations down under with the same macabre resentment and fascination we had towards elephantiasis, picking apart the steps and analyzing the underlying biological vulnerability (most often dating back all the way to Eve and that damn piece of fruit), cross-referencing the tell-tale signs with previous cases, believing that the hearts of men could be solved with the right amount of praying or tinkering or prayerful tinkering.

Only Emily poked at her uncut piece while moving her mouth, bubbles forming at the corner of her lips. Emily lived below me, on the second floor of the Haste, and although both she and her roommate, Edna, had the same prepubescent voice, soft, slightly shrill, like a cat mewing in earnest over some lost hairball, or yarn, I liked her anyway. Some evenings I'd stalk on Emily's couch and eat her miniature Teddy Grahams. She always had a box handy.

"The mini ones always taste different than the full-size ones," she told me.

"Different how?" I said.

She giggled. "Different better."

"Want some?" I offered, even though they were hers to begin with.

"Maybe later," she said, eyeing the ones in my hand with the same look I used to throw at home-owning Kaiser techs at church.

In the middle of spring semester, Emily disappeared.

"Where's Emily?" I asked Edna. She had just told me that Eugene and Matt both told her that they thought I was a "super godly woman," which was really just a few verbs away from being a marriage proposal, and for a brief moment I thought we could be friends.

"Emily, she's on a mental health vacation," Edna said, laugh-coughing.

"What the hell does that mean?"

Edna leaned in, conspiratorially. "She's at an institution."

"We're at an institution," I said. "It's called the University of California."

"Well, this one is in Arizona," she said.

"She switched schools?"

"She's in rehab."

"What, drugs?" I asked. It could never be drugs.

"No, Teddy Grahams," she said. I laughed before I saw the arches of Edna's eyebrows pulling the rest of her girlish, brown face up, drooping against gravity to condemn me for my levity.

"You're serious," I observed.

"Am I ever funny?" she asked. Ironically and for a moment, she was.

The next week all the women at Haste got together and wrote cards for Emily. I found a sea green piece of card stock and wrote in wormlike cursive, "We make plans. God laughs." It was supposed to be uplifting, but in retrospect I could see how it sounded a bit dark, existential even, all things considered.

By fall, Emily was back.

"How was it?" I asked, trying to be noncommittal about it.

Emily smiled with only her eyes this time; her mouth didn't move. "Well, I'm back," she said, as if there was some protection from stating the obvious. I eyed her exposed pantry for Teddy Grahams and did not spot any.

"Joyce Meyers says we eat when we're emotional," I said. "Anything you want to talk about?"

"What's new with you?" she asked instead.

"BT told me, 'I wish you would stay here forever,' after Salsa Night at church," I said. "But he didn't ask me to dance."

Emily nodded and adjusted her shoulders.

"I wrote a poem about that on my blog, and why forever never means what it sounds like. The IP address tracker picked up that he read it."

"What are you going to do?" Emily said.

"I saw him on Sunday after the sermon and ran in the other direction. Now I'm fasting about the whole thing."

I looked at her to see if she would take the bait. "You fasting too?"

"You're sweet," she said.

"Seriously though. What happened over there?"

Emily looked around, and I wondered if she noticed the missing grahams. Finally, she said, "They gave out Skittles, one at a time, whenever we said something really deep and meaningful at group therapy."

"They gave out candy at a clinic for eating disorders?"

"The Skittles were mainly for the anorexics. You know, like a gateway drug, to get them to start eating again."

"Did it work?"

"They didn't force-feed us or anything. People did what they wanted with the Skittle."

"What's there to do with a Skittle other than pop it in your mouth?"

"You have multiple holes, you know. It's small enough to fit anywhere, really."

I didn't ask whether she was talking about her nostril, or somewhere else; exploring holes would be something that came later, after the heart cookies were long gone.

"What did you do?"

"With the Skittle?"

"With anything."

"I went on all the field trips."

"That sounds progressive."

"Well, it was to the grocery store."

"Never mind. Sounds like punishment then."

"More like a barometer," Emily said. "For measuring our progress."

"I don't get it."

"We'd practice walking up and down the aisles."

"What was the test?"

"To see if you could hold it together."

I always liked grocery stores; every visit was like a Vegas convention—the displays lurid, the workers incompetent and nonchalant, the opportunities for consumption endless. Every time Mommy announced she was going, I'd jump up from whatever I was doing — fractions, piano practice, Garfield cartoons — and tag along. Getting two dollars each week to pick one box of breakfast-themed goods was just the surface of it; I always resolved to attend to every aisle, making special note of the new items on the end caps and clearance products ear-marked orange in the back. It all felt very pimp, getting to check things out and finger them before putting them back without consequence or measure. At first it seemed wrong to fondle each individual peach, but it was so mundane that eventually it felt right. I wondered what Emily felt.

"Could you do it?" I asked.

"Sometimes," she said.

The following Saturday, I offered to drive us both to to the grocery store. "I've got to get more water," I said. "And those taquitos everyone likes."

"Come with me?" I said, after she did not hear the question implicit in the announcement.

"I'm not sure if that's a good idea," she said.

"It's just practice," I said. "You don't have to buy anything. I'll assist," I promised. I meant I'd help her eat whatever she couldn't finish before the expiration date. She must've thought I meant something else.

Emily and I held hands when we walked across the parking lot; it was one of those innocent habits we picked up during a mission trip from girls in China who held each other's hands everywhere they went, as if stuck together by some unbreakable platonic force. We liked the idea and practiced it all over the Bay Area, throwing off all the lesbians with our straight girl talk of boys at church. I held my membership card in my palm and flashed it at the bald man stationed at the entrance.

Once inside, the fluorescent rods illuminated every surface with a stark, veneer-like sheen; even the microfiber onesies by the door seemed to flicker as if caught in some resplendent Monet painting of poppies on the side of a hill. Emily walked behind me while squinting at the packages stacked in every direction.

"You okay there?" I asked.

"I'm on Ativan," she said, sounding harassed.

"Is it working?" I said. I learned about Ativan the semester prior: a benzodiazepine, used to produce a calming effect on your central nervous system.

She watched a woman pushing a cart full of cokes and biscotti, wheels crackling with the weight of all the aluminum and carbonation. Then she said, "Maybe you go on without me."

"I'm not leaving you in the middle of Costco," I said. "We'll never find each other again."

"We have phones."

"You never answer yours." I could tell I was right because she did not offer a rebuttal.

"Let's go to the back," I said. "Taquitos and water."

"Taquitos and water," Emily repeated, her voice small, like a pet's.

Things started to fall apart in produce. "Those tomatoes look like they're made out of Pyrex," I said. "Makes you wonder, doesn't it?"

"I hate them," Emily said, staring intently at the fruits.

"We're not getting any," I promised.

"I'm stuffed," she replied. "I had this huge muffin for breakfast. It probably counted as two muffins, really. That's the issue with these places. One is really two, and two means it's over; you're done with already."

"You're fine," I said, steering us away from the uniformed lady microwaving bagel bites. "No one is being ruined here."

Emily ducked into the refrigerated section reserved for the fussy produce—leafy greens or thin-skinned fruits prone to bruising and drooping—and squeezed her two hands together. "This is crazy," she said. "Who eats this much salad?"

"Quit it," I said.

She stretched her eyes open with both sets of fingers and looked past me at the shoppers honoring the ancient tradition of hunting and gathering, just without the hunt and needless caloric expenditure, perceiving that the new order of the universe involved — invariably — food upon endless food and being potbellied in shorts. She looked at me; appeared to decide that I was part of the conspiracy. "No one needs fucking taquitos," she said.

"What about the water?" I countered. It didn't matter. I had separated my friend from her weak hold on equilibrium — and over what? Frozen Mexican? I placed both my hands on her forearms and applied pressure, a dumb tech using gentle squeezing to staunch an exploded aorta, as if the world could be saved if only we gave out more hugs.

Emily, she had been tracing the outline of my face with her eyes. When she reached my chin she smiled softly and dream-like. I asked her what was wrong; I said I was sorry and admitted to being an idiot of the most unforgivable kind — the kind who saw it coming. I shook her a little, hard, like a bad mom, trusting full well that the first aid would never work but might look good after the fact, a brownie point on the autopsy report. It's the end of the world and the robots are coming, sang the song in my head, the one we made up on blank afternoons during missions when there was nothing to do but hold hands.

"Resistance is futile," she said finally, her cheeks wet and inflamed like those of a child, lost in a grocery store.

EXCEPTION

The most gentle thing is the empty chair
      next to you. A space I could wish in-
to. Today the leaves are wormed with yellow
      against the blue skies' fresh, infested
with a cool, so I think *Fall* — the season
      and the action. This afternoon, oh,
how I imagined a walk with you, since
      being in love makes a poet one.
Yet we check our pulses, with our own hands;
      I recall your elsewhere apartment.
When I chose this mountain landscape, could I
      tell how distance would rot, mar itself.
My room here two arm spans wide; too much,
      though I like exceeding, except like this.

EVERYTHING IMAGINED THAT WAS

I.
no parent wishes for haunting
        an overhang of stalactite daggers
atmospheric grief   tents
        every move

nostalgia
        this mind disease eats flesh
walking rememory
                silent blur

        on the film reel
        the blanked scenes define me —
                                arm against foliage   a dog
                a young self   running
the now self   reaches

a screen keeps me out

that self attempts to touch
        mirage
                recollection   i keep racing the track
peer around ongoing corners
        i stretch for breath or reply
someone to solidify   memory
        i beg a firmness to confirm constriction
a candle contained by glass
parking lot light dulled by the night
envelope of time sealed by fog

give me constraint from touching
        that which drives me to touch

II.
silent wall
        i negotiate aloneness in sleep
words of a song spin into fruition:
        the winter does come
               (we have not yet escaped February)
        the lover does leave
               (my grey sheets are wholly mine)

i touch his arm as he hovers —
a still — above me — isolated shot
skin against lips   my pores spill over
he drifts to the coast   again
our pacific longings   shall not
    be
        discussed

BÀ NỘI RESTS AT SEA

I.
Bà nội, the water rises. What once worried me
was never finding you. The grass grown high,
a cemetery, a mile-long walk from which direction
I don't know. My father asks a neighbor, help
with your headstone's location. Another neighbor
shrugs. The sun presses, calls out
sweat. Slip. My back. Curved
vertebrae of relative
links. We find the marked circle, your body's
sphere, wipe the stone, light the stick, bow
with incense. The dead trace us,
a perforated line forever tied, not always
tight. My father wounds the twine. His
secret layers many faces much guilt
seeps I stand in sun water rises

II.
Seawater laps against inland hills. Oil rigs falter as they
will as we will. Plastics new
factories South China Sea drilling heats homes
water rises surrounding rice paddies salt
grain cellar parched a dry mouth a moth
upturned you are always home even wilted
grasses perpetual flood covered stone sanitized
traces your breath on cement
against the pitch of a country
night crickets echo ripples a new
sea level

JENNIFER CONLON

MOM'S BOYFRIENDS

This one was called Best Fuck.
We weren't quite sure what that meant,
but he did have a non-threatening smile
like Mr. Rogers. He always brought bags of Skittles.
The only time he ever raised his voice
was at night when mom said YES. YES.
The headboard smacking against my wall, thick
screams through the air vent. YES.
Brother suggested stuffing the vent with a pillow,
but mom and Best Fuck were coming through
the walls. When he stopped coming around, mom drank
nothing but Strawberry Slim Fast for two weeks,
got fired at her job for attacking her boss during a meeting,
and demanded more child support. But I could sleep now.
I always slept best in the space between
boyfriends. I slept sound, even through her woody voice
telling us it was our fault Best Fuck wasn't coming
back. He said our sad little eyes turned him off.

HOUSE FIRE

Miss Jones leads us to the auditorium
where Firefighter Man stands
by a miniature wood house.

In this scenario my parent is Miss Jones
who dotes outside the window, insists
I not get discouraged as my house
burns me out of it.

A boy barges forward,
asks if we will get to see a firetruck today
and he is promised yes.

We are asked to pretend
the house is on fire and it's not hard
because they've painted believable flames
over the doors and licking up windows.

Firefighter Man shows us how to test
orange-painted door knobs for heat
and how to get from the bed to the window

alive with such small fingers.
Alive like the fire and the house and Miss Jones.
This house is like my grandma's, small
shelter for a wild animal and its descendants.

The doorway burns brilliant and bows to the weight
of the house. The house wants to live. It curls
and glows and holds me in its closet. Miss Jones

and Firefighter Man and barging boy all shouting
for me to get out. The boy is laughing at the flare
licking up my pink windbreaker pants.
Doesn't she know it's not real? It's a full house.

Everyone is watching me move like a planet
between rooms. The kitchen has its own imagination.
I shout back at barging boy *Of course it's real!*
Why do you think the firetrucks are here?

My grandma is in the kitchen pouring ginger ale
into a yellow sippy cup. She holds me
better than the closet, better than

Miss Jones' hand reaching in through the window,
her long manicured nails
catching flame like little matchsticks. How
could I ever save them?

HEADLANDS

It began one year ago when he could no longer write his name onto a piece of paper. He was signing the back of a check he'd received from one of his students when Preston Deene recognized that he had trouble holding the pen in his grasp.

It was the end of the term and the check was for a telescope that he had purchased at the start of the school year for one of his most inspiring students. The girl didn't have much money, and neither did he, but she refused to accept the telescope unless he promised to allow her to reimburse him for half of the cost. He reluctantly agreed and hoped that she might forget to pay the debt by the end of the term. She did not, and he knew she wouldn't.

"Is everything okay, Mr. Deene?" she asked as she watched him sign the check with considerable difficulty. Preston observed his shaking hand. He'd felt certain light tremors in his extremities over the last few weeks, but nothing quite like this.

"I think so, Susan," he replied. "Seems like a little motor neuron issue going on here. Frayed nerves." He grinned. "Serves me right for signing this check before getting to the bank. Bad habit of mine. My mother used to scold me for it on birthdays."

Susan studied his hand as if it were resting on a petri dish.

"Maybe go see a doctor? Please?"

"Ah, Susan, it's nothing to worry about." He slipped the check into his pocket unsigned. "Is the telescope still working out for you? Did you catch that spectacular glimpse of Jupiter over the weekend?"

Susan perked up.

"I did! It was so beautiful." She placed her hand on her textbook. "I really don't mind microbiology, it's fine and all, but

I can't wait to take your astronomy course next year. By then, I'll have really mastered that telescope."

"I'm looking forward to it, too, but don't forget that to fully understand the largest things in the universe, you should first understand the smallest. Tiny molecules and particles make up even the most complicated objects."

"Right, I know, Mr. Deene. I bet Jupiter itself is such a cosmopolitan mix of odd elements."

"I don't just mean the biggest things either. If you can understand the items in this textbook, then you'll have an edge in understanding the most mysterious object in all the cosmos," he said as he tapped the side of his head with his index finger. "Use it in good health, Susan."

She smiled at him.

A week later, Preston had his first visit with a doctor.

Within a few months, the symptoms had grown worse. Even the specialists were surprised at how fast it was progressing. Preston began dropping things left and right; he broke a toe after dropping a gallon of milk onto his foot. After his second fall down the stairs, he took a leave of absence from the school, much to Susan's shock and dismay. They still met occasionally for coffee to discuss her studies and to converse about the stars, but she need no longer study him like a rat in a maze to know that something was terribly wrong. His voice wavered and he mumbled at times.

One day, he received a call from his neurologist informing him that they had finally made a diagnosis. He hoped it was Parkinson's. Preston had read everything that he could find regarding his symptoms and knew that it was likely one of two things. His old college roommate had been diagnosed with Parkinson's about a decade earlier and though he knew his friend's life had been forever altered after his diagnosis, the man was still alive — still working and making a small difference in the world. The other possible diagnosis was too treacherous to consider.

Susan drove him to his appointment since Preston had no living family or close friends who were aware of his situation. During the ride, she often turned to him and observed him — he knew she was too curious and too clever not to have done her own research into his symptoms, as well. He did not mention that he would soon learn his fate, but rather that he was just heading in for a checkup. She dropped him off and agreed to return in an hour.

Preston's doctor knew that his patient was well-aware of what he would face no matter which diagnosis he delivered. This didn't make breaking the news to him any easier and neither did the fact that he had grown quite fond of Preston's soft-spoken nature and pleasant demeanor. His physician asked him to sit down in the wooden chair opposite his desk, which groaned as Preston lowered himself onto it.

"Preston, I'm afraid it's ALS." The doctor couldn't look him in the eye. After thirty-seven years of practicing medicine, it was one of only a handful of times that he could not muster the strength to do so.

"Amyotrophic lateral sclerosis," Preston said while looking at his unsteady hands. "I suppose we can't hide it with initialism."

The doctor pushed the paperwork to the side.

"Sometimes, this is the worst job in the world." He pursed his lips. "Preston, I'm truly sorry."

Susan pulled up to the curb outside the office. She offered to help Preston into the car, but he refused. Before she could ask how the checkup went, he began to talk about Jupiter. He talked on and on about how it was a gas giant comprised mainly of hydrogen and helium, how it contained two and a half times the mass of all the other planets in the solar system combined. She looked over from time to time and nodded, never smiling, as if jotting notes in a classroom setting.

From that point on, Preston and Susan communicated solely through letters. He took out his old Olivetti Lettera and found the slow hammering of the keys meditative. Though his letters were pocked with typing errors, he blamed it on the timeworn machine and added in a note that it contributed a distinctive character to his correspondence. Susan had found her family's vintage Underwood in a basement closet and relished typing out letters and anxiously awaiting a reply in the mail.

After a few months, Preston's letters arrived only sparingly. In one of his last, he mentioned that he had some bad news.

The Headlands is a dark sky park located at the northernmost tip of Michigan's lower peninsula, just a short drive off I-75 in Mackinaw City before the bridge. There one will find 550-acres of preserved land set aside solely for viewing the ancient sky at night. There are a handful of dark sky parks across the country, but the Headlands was always Preston's favorite. He had spent many summer nights there as a child with his family, and it was there that he had fostered his love for the wide-open expanse, filled with worlds that resided beyond.

Preston was on a bus headed north toward Mackinaw City. Susan had driven him to the station and nearly wept when she saw his debilitated condition, though she hid her emotions well. When she asked where he was headed, he only said that he was planning to visit some old friends. When she asked who they were, he told her about how the Milky Way galaxy is mostly comprised of dark matter, and appears quite flat, like a disc, from a distance. But because of this dark matter, he added, it also possesses an invisible halo of concealed luminous matter that cannot be seen by the naked eye, wielding it into a warped form, the halo ever-present around it. Susan looked over at him.

"You see, even in darkness, there is some light," he said. "Even when there appears to be nothing, there is something."

For much of the bus ride, he thought about his future. He was relieved that Susan had not asked about his lack of luggage when she dropped him off. It had been a year since his symptoms first appeared and he knew if he was lucky, he might have a year left, give or take. But he also knew that remaining time would not be pleasant. Without a loved one or family to help care for him, he would be relegated to the hands of a nursing facility. As he always suspected he might, he now somewhat regretted never finding a partner — someone to have and to hold, for better or worse, for now would come the worse.

Dying from the complications of ALS is near the top in terms of the most horrifying deaths, he thought. After you've gone through the struggles of feeling your muscles erode, your speech and mobility fade, and once your hollow shell has been plopped onto a cot in some bleached white room somewhere, you simply await the final step: the eventual cessation of breathing, breath by breath, as you lie awake, fully aware and acutely conscious of the fact *that this is it.*

Miracles can happen. Take Stephen Hawking, for instance, Preston thought. The man had survived for more than forty years with this illness. And though it makes for a touching story — and one that he cherished as Hawking was a personal hero of his — he also knew the reality: hardly anyone survives for very long with ALS. But to him, Hawking wasn't human in any regard. On top of that, the amount of support that the celebrated scientist received (and deserved) was paramount. He knew that there would be no salvation for him to count on, no league of saviors to rush to his aid. Hawking was the exception rather than the rule — the hidden halo of light in the vast, foreboding dark. More than ninety percent of the universe remains in the dark matter, yet, without it, nothing in the vast expanse of space could function. There would always be exceptions, but Preston knew he was not exceptional; he was the constant.

As a boy, looking up at the night sky in the Headlands, he was first exposed to true wonder. Any child gazing off into that wide abyss cannot help but sense an intoxicating sentiment of a dynamic size and sheer possibility — pure pulchritude. There was no fear out in space for Preston. The unknown was simply that: unknown. Nothing else mattered, save for what he saw above and felt in his heart.

He thanked and paid the taxi driver who had dropped him off at the Headlands. The man asked if Preston needed any help carrying his bag, but Preston declined. He'd put everything that he would need into one backpack and slipped it over his shoulders. It would be an arduous journey to his old spot in the park that he treasured so dearly, but he knew he would make it.

The trek took a lot out of him and he stopped frequently to rest along the way, watching the big dipper fireflies hovering serenely through the swaying blades of marram grass. It was growing dark and being a weekday, he was alone. When he finally reached the spot, he recognized it instantly. A stump with a wide, flat surface was nearby and he set his backpack down next to it. With enormous effort, he pulled the Olivetti Lettera out from the bag and set it onto the stump. Then he leaned back and collapsed onto the soft dirt, fireflies buzzing lazily around his head, pulsating with a minute glow. It was dusk and the sky was fading from a brilliant azure into an inviting vermillion, as if the sun itself had scorched the heavens above. Soon the atmosphere would transfigure into total blackness — an all-encompassing reminder of the dark matter that bound our universe together.

Many people facing the end hope to see the whole wide world before they die, or perhaps some small, specific part of it, but Preston had little interest in that. His focus was on casting his eyes on the cosmos above.

After he had watched the sky transition above him, Preston Deene took four candles out of his backpack in the final moments of the waning dusk. He placed them onto the stump next to the typewriter's four corners. He lit each one carefully, making sure it provided enough light to see the paper in the reel, and pushed the spent matches into the soil burnt end first. Then he rubbed his trembling hands, preparing to type.

He wanted to be honest with Susan, but also realized that it might be difficult for her to understand his decision. Many of

71

their conversations after his diagnosis had been dominated by his conscious need to change the subject. In the end, he knew she might have already figured everything out. What he now hoped to do with this letter was to cast some of her own brilliance into the gloomy time soon to come. In writing the letter, he wished to illuminate the situation not only for her, but to attain some semblance of a conclusion for himself, as well.

He began the letter by thanking her for all her help throughout the last year. Without her, he wrote, much of what he was able to accomplish would have otherwise been impossible; the most important of these was none other than keeping a positive outlook toward the future. Though he knew his story was drawing to a close, he felt heartened that there, in his own classroom, he'd been lucky enough to help uncover a talented young woman who would one day grow up to do astonishing things. And though he knew she was capable of so many wide-ranging possibilities, be it in science or policymaking, he stressed to her that none of that really mattered unless she was content in her own skin. If she chose to live in a diving bell at the bottom of the ocean, then that would be fine, so long as she didn't lament her place there. He told her of a coming age when humankind might be able to leave Earth and explore the surrounding worlds, but whether she merely took notes while gazing through her telescope, or became the first person to set foot on Mars mattered not, so long as it was a decision that she made with all her heart.

He told her that she would make plenty of choices that she might regret, as everyone, including himself, often does. If she was sitting alone in her diving bell and felt sick with grief, or watched eagerly as others rose through the clouds in massive ships made of carbon — the same carbon that brought Columbus over the oceans and allowed Magellan to circumnavigate the planet — then all she need do is change her course. The universe was a sea of possibility.

In the closing of the letter, he revealed his prognosis and the full extent of his disease. He asked her not to think of him as she read his words, but just the words themselves. Someday, he wrote, there could come a time when she or someone she loved might face the type of future that he now faced, and when that time came, all that would be important was what she had learned up to that point; the elucidations resting in what she'd done, where she'd been, and how she changed the people and things she touched in those places. Though everything comes to an end at one point or another, there's little use in getting to any conclusion at all if the story itself wasn't worth much. He ended the letter: *Be sure to find your own halo in the darkness of your universe. Strive to be the exception to any rule that you don't wish to follow.*

Typing those final words, Preston understood that he had not wasted his life. He suddenly remembered all the exceptional individuals that he had met throughout the years, realizing that he had not only touched their lives, but that they had touched his in a similar fashion, and he could fondly remember the lessons learned from teachers of his own. No life is wasted spent guiding others along their voyage.

After he finished typing the letter, he rubbed his shaking hands for more than a few minutes. He took out an envelope from the bag, slipped in the folded pages, and sealed it. Upon the letter he carefully wrote Susan's name and next to it drew a crude rendition of Jupiter as best he could. He inserted the letter into his interior jacket pocket and then carefully blew out each of the candles one by one until he was consumed by the darkness surrounding him, the way a cave-black moon overtakes the sun during an eclipse.

He looked up and saw that the Milky Way was bright and filled the high expanse above like the wide path of some misbegotten explorer — a ship's vibrant wake cut out across an ocean of white, twinkling lights. There was hardly any room for darkness in the sky above the Headlands, as nothing could remain hidden by the obfuscating haze of man's influence; what you saw out here was real and unimpeachable.

Preston laid out onto the soft earth below him, shaking, and reached over into his bag and felt for a small plastic bottle. He took a large handful of its contents, dropping a few from his trembling hands, and put them all into his mouth. He sat up a bit in order to swallow, taking a long drink of water. After that, he leaned back and began to count the stars—billions and billions of them—one by one.

REILLY D. COX

AT THE CONTRACEPTION MUSEUM

after E

1. *Intrauterine devices*

T-shaped device inserted into the uterus.

Known as an IUD or coil, in reference to coiled construction.

Note: Imagine coiling.

1909, first reported success by an IUD or coil.

Note: Oh, Rebecca.

Later improved by Dr. Gräfenberg, of G-spot fame.

Note: studies began in the 1940s.

Due to materials at hand and skill of the maker, constructions result in strange and varied appearances.

Note: a wedding ring.

Note: sea creatures, known and imagined.

Note: pinned butterflies. The appearance of. Arizona, checkerspots. Dull firetips. American ladies. Maryland, monarchs. Fritallaries.

Cloudless sulphurs.

My mother turns to autumn beside the IUDs.

Note: this is not the same as weeping.

She walks down the aisle towards the wall of copper wire, of homemade butterflies —

studies her reflection in the glass, etching wings back into her —

begging the tiny wings to flutter.

Note: how she turns to autumn.

When you try to draw her attention to the next exhibit, the abortifacient flowers, she stops you, says, I already know.

2.   *Abortifacient flowers*

Common Rue. Pennyroyal. Wild Carrot.
Blue Cohosa. Mugwort. The girls
my mother plays hooky to meet near the creek.
They tease her for her uniform, ask if the nuns
know she's out, pull her back, *no no,*
we're being silly. A few of the girls begin
undressing and climb into the creek. *It's better*
as a tea, they say, *but this will do.* The remaining
girls approach my mother, beckon her to open wide.
You have some trouble, the girls say. *Let me help.*

3. *Alligator dung*

Emerging from the creek,
an alligator carries my unconscious mother

to shore. *Tsk, tsk* — the alligator's
hiss. *What am I to do with you*

when you're like this? Blonde hair
dragging through the water

attracts fish, which the alligator
is quick to shoo away.

The alligator, at the shore, rolls
my mother through mud, hides

her in tall grasses. Waking, she finds
the sun has baked her, impenetrable.

At home, her mother asks, *What boy*
will want you with muddied socks?

But my mother keeps from cracking,
knows nothing's getting in now.

4. *Cervical caps and diaphragms*

My mother is in the kitchen slicing Florida Shine #9 Oranges
for cervical caps. She lines them in rows along the window sill,
hands them to girls on their way to morning classes, wishes
them well. She finds me napping underneath the checkered
table with half an orange in my mouth and grain in my shoes,
scolds me for my selfishness. *Now Ruth has no protection.*

What will she do? She reaches through the window, gleans
an orange off the tree, begins slicing. *You know,* she says,
they say that Casanova used lemons as cervical caps
for his women. You knew which women were his by the scent.

5. *Early literature*

James Ashton's *The Book of Nature.*

> Note: the hand-colored plates, the illustrations. You can
> see right inside the women. As if to say, This is where
> the garden grows. *Don't step here, or here. Your boot*
> *prints will become flower beds.*

6. *Condoms*

Fashion me a sleeve of linen. Dive into the creek and come up
with a fish's bladder. If you find yourself gutless, take a sheep's
gut. Now come here, little artist boy, and touch me. Touch me
without touching me.

7. *Sponges*

Diving to the bottom of the sea,
I find a reef. I know how to hide

my blonde hair beneath a cap.
I know how not to knick my fingertips

on the coral. This salt-sweet pressure
is heavy satin. I can hold my breath

for years, for this. At last, I find it,
and return to land with a sea sponge.

I whisper sweet nothings to it,
promise not to place it in boiling water,

or you might shrink! No, later
I'll soak you in a vinegar bath

and hide you in a safe place —
such a safe, small space. I swear.

8.   *Female medicines*

For ladies in a certain situation,
steep this in a tea. Take from its tin,
unfold it, and read it delicately.
If you like, sweeten it with wintergreen
or, if you prefer, spearmint. To induce
a stoppage of nature, take this, and wait.
Now, for those other ladies, those
ladies believing they are in a family way,
set this down. Shut your mouth tightly.
Even if your husband commands you, *open.*

9.   *Early Literature*

Aristotle's Masterpiece, Displaying the Secrets of Man in the Generation
of Man

> Note: Aristotle's problems: *Can you tell me how to tie my*
> *shoes in my bedchamber? the secret to being a good gardener?*
> *the way a child can grow into anything but a weed?*

10. *Oral contraceptive pills*

My mother and her sister find themselves carried away to a great feast in Mexico City. A table. The ground, littered with hundreds of yams. My mother, lovely in dirt, grabbed at the roots, gorged herself into slumber. My mother woke three days wrapped in a bright blanket. Yellow over orange. A streak of red. The border, purple as Sunday. Her sister smiling over her. *How are you feeling, little sister? How are you feeling?*

11. *Early Literature*

Robert Dale Owen's *Moral Physiology, or, A brief and plain treatise on the population question*

> Note: Practice like the French do. When a dog barks, clap three times above your head. Take precautions when dealing with Englishmen and keep the feather of a young crow in your cap. Remember that the legs are the greatest source of pleasure, as they carry us to such pleasure, and should be thanked and damned accordingly. For those without the use of legs, the damning and blessing of wheels should suffice. Doubt any advice given by persons born in 1831. And most importantly — note this — when reaching that moment of greatest joy, pull away from your lover, and sleep.

12. *Rhythm method*

Note: we are different from animals. That is the first problem.

13. *Douching and spermicides*

At the end of a long pier, my mother becomes a fish
for my father to hurl into waves. When my father
points at me for 'next,' my mother surfaces, tries
to negotiate, forgetting that my father does not

speak fish. I am the son who cannot ride a bicycle,
the son who cannot dive off a long pier, and he
is going to teach me today, dammit. My mother,
seeing that she cannot dissuade my father, looks
up at me with her compact, fishy eyes and says,

God is a tiny creature hiding at the bottom
of the ocean. This is how we find them. With that,
my father rips my legs out from beneath me,
and I swear I can feel my back breaking, or,
and this is small, I feel a certain kind of love.

OF THE DUST

no need to be pretty if you are good girl,
bush hair escaping from colorful barrettes
masking mud child underneath

when i was a little girl i folded into myself
swallowed the width of my belly whole
mixing watercolors with clay to create chaos.

it was birthright to live and die in ayiti,
unsung hallelujahs written on disposable things
mother mud girl mother good

there was no need for childhoods
candy sneaking into pockets at corner store
bubble gum lip things behind the library
permission to go down slide in chanmas
permission to teary eyed

i left parts of my mud girl in port-au-prince
where my stomach ate itself for fourteen nights
and in the sky is where i buried her
shy girl in dalmation shirt outed
at at seven as woman in chanmas

underneath the heavy i was mud child
shaping rice in the palm of my hands
so my pieces where easier to lose
and not for nothing
i was home

POST QUARANTINE REVELATIONS

the bibles were the last thing to be burned
psalms like fireflies into the night sky
and they told us to be patient

fixed our hands into our pockets so we could have something
        to hold onto before the flood
before the levees broke in the presence of a blue moon
and we wondered where the babies went

where they're bodies called momma when our bodies could no
        longer fix the broken things

there's no more space on this island for my burning breasts
for my grandmother's dying breast
for my grandma's unfixed eyes

i have broken the bloodline of my body so there's nothing to
        take
nothing to salvage within my wreckage and i can walk now
raise my nose at the burning of man's flesh
as i caress a deadman's ear in my pocket

what a waste of a body when we are no longer interested in
        making it feel used

AMONG OTHER THINGS,
GOD IS A WOMAN

bring me to where my blood runs—
where my mouth rants like cockatoo
and america admits she is stubborn.
the whole world rests at my tongue to be
examined, soothed, then swallowed on a
sunday in the middle of market.
you haven't brought me home yet.
back to bush unburned and rooted.
i am made to reflect god, and she is woman.
full bodied and loud and holding your daddy's
feelings in a closet with a box of dice.
she shakes and blows and death drops
and gambles on black and ugly
and centered and i live.

I-80E

At the Travel Oasis off I-80, Jesus washes Peter's feet in the bed of a rust-eaten Chevy. They are carved together. The cab is empty. A mile off, near Elkhart, Indiana, a storm huffs upward like a wave, ready to spit lightning, rain, and wind. Ready to beat cars below, scatter travelers inside.

The outside wall of the Travel Oasis is swirl brick, the pattern of sandstone or port wine cheese spread, with tall mirror windows. An American flag, ripped long between the middle stripes, flaps on a pole along the front walk. A high school dance team in matching charcoal sweatshirts and mismatched neon hair, yawn and amble toward a minivan wordless, carrying Chex Mix and Monster energy drinks. A trio of Greek women in yoga pants, beaded shirts, all dark eyed and long curled hair, talk with their hands and perfectly done nails. Travelers cross the lot. Some stop to observe Jesus and Peter in the Chevy, to admire their dark grace. Most do not.

A Mennonite elder leans on the wall besides the entrance. A black stallion horse hair hat rests on his head. His beard grows down from his chin, orange and white like a falling fire. His pants are short, pulled tight around his waist. He stands next to an ashtray, a squeaky metal trapdoor on a pedestal made of small smooth stones. He looks out. The statue is big, he notes, they are just bigger than normal people. A yellow strap is pulled across Jesus' back and around Peter's waist. They aren't going anywhere but it feels like rain.

The reflective green sign on the highway advertises Burger King and Pizza Hut Express, which is only part true. The Burger King is open for business but the Pizza Hut is just a dead hole, a blighted-out space, filled with metal chairs and dusty restaurant equipment. The food court is clean enough but smells like ancient gasoline and the blood under fingernails. Local news plays on a muted television mounted high. Some crane their heads with mild interest. Pixelated masses of orange and red move across the weather map. Some kid, just out of college, walks back and forth, as the masses slide and twist behind him.

The screen cuts to an anchor, wearing a pink blazer, brown skin and straight hair. Her mouth moves, eyes locked to the camera. Closed Captioning, disrupted by the storm, rolls out chunky, white text within black boxes: NEWS TODAY INNN DECADE OLD**-LD CASE KHEART CNTY DETECTIVES EXHUME REMAINS JANE DOE, DSCOVERD HUNTRS 1996 - DETECTVES NEW EVDNE%% DNA BRING CLOSER TO FINDING VCTMS IDENTITYY. The camera cuts to archival VHS footage: a field in winter. Men in navy blue windbreakers inside a grove of trees wrapped on all sides with flapping yellow police tape.

Few watch the screen. The janitor, white hair and grey skin scuffs his work boots across the floor. All day, all week, all year he moves through bodies. Legs and shoulders, glossy driving eyes and open silent mouths, slumping toward the bathroom, sitting in the stalls, washing their hands, buying burgers and Gummy Bears. Eating, excreting and returning to their cars. He has smiled at folks in the past, spoken niceties, is not afraid to making himself known. Though he is sometimes embarrassed how his jaw waggles, skinny on the side where the tumor was. But he has his own friends. This is just his job after all, and these people won't be staying long. However, he thinks, leaning on his broom, watching from the food court: that man just outside the bathroom hallway has been here for some time.

Excuse me? The man says as people enter and exit the bathroom. He bloats in the middle and has stickly limbs. A diabetic turnip. He sometimes leans on an aluminum metal cane, its foam handle brown and cracked from use. Thick glasses slide down his nose.

Excuse me, can I ask you for help?

A biker wearing a shaved head, wraparound sunglasses, a motorcycle t-shirt cut free of sleeves and open almost to his waist, scoffs. A young father in sweatpants and an AC/DC t-shirt carries his yapping toddler, a boy with long blonde hair and shiny eyes, quickly past to avoid the interaction all together. A large Asian family sharing food from Styrofoam containers, taking up four tables in the dining area, disregards him when he walks over. Excuse me, can I ask you for help? They don't allow the question. The man keeps smiling and asking. His combover coming undone as he shakes with each gesture of helplessness, his clothes loosen, his teeth loosen, his eyes grow wilder in his head. He's in and out like static and barely exists.

Excuse me?

The janitor walks outside to get away from him, bringing his broom, though he doesn't intend to use it. He slides atop a picnic bench in an enclave to the side of the building, where wind and trash get trapped and swirl lazily together. The air is thick. He takes off his glasses and polishes the cracked lenses on the bottom of his shirt. On the highway, cars, trucks and motorcycles fling around a big corner, fresh off the Chicago Tollway Bridge. Before that they came through Gary. Where wires hang like a network of scars, where the carcasses of steel mills and stacks blooming smoke like true death line the road.

The janitor watches blurry vehicles race into the storm, then looks back at the lot. He gasps. Who are these giants in the bed of that pickup? He puts his glasses back on. No. His mind clicks back into place. He cranes his head. Even from that distance, he can see the swirl in the woodgrain on Peter's shoulder, he can see the streak and shine in the varnish of Jesus' hair. It could rain any minute. He looks back inside the building where the shadows of travelers mix, morph and move behind the mirror glass. Stats, the ones and twos from the days baseball games dissolve and are replaced on the screen in the food court. He does not see the man who was coming undone and asking for help. The janitor touches the dip in his jaw.

Behind him now, facing a brick pillar, a woman rocks and prays clutching a black book, no bigger than a cassette tape. Sleeves and a knit cap cover her. Her dress is striped, bright pink, blue, and purple. The pillar is pocked with ash where cigarettes have been put out against it. A few feet away the young father in the AC/CD t-shirt scolds his son for grabbing cigarette butts spilled out of an ashtray tower. The praying woman does not open her eyes. Her lips move and offer only a hum. Roots of words, but not words.

The son yaps and yaps, wearing a pair of his father's boxer shorts, cinched with a hair tie, (because he peed his pants in the car) and golden sparkly shoes. He laughs as cigarette butts, some smeared with dark red lipstick, are pried from his fingers. The father shushes the ash off his child's hands and they stroll up next to the picnic table where the janitor is sitting. The son starts to jump off the curb into the lot. The father snatches him under the armpit—Seriously?! You do not walk into the parking lot alone!

The father smiles embarrassed at the janitor, rolls his eyes and picks up his son. Lightning flashes across the sky, like a god ripping the page. The father winces, a horror dream playing in his head. On the road, rain covering the windshield faster than wipers can push it away. Hydroplaning, being sucked under the sharp middle of a semi-trailer. The father imagines their life inside a twisted wreck, like a beer can stomped off center.

Across the highway, where an identical structure once stood there is nothing, just leveled ground and sleeping dozers. Are they remodeling this place too? The father gestures to the oasis.

It won't be here much longer, the janitor says between drags, a taste of rotten fruit welling in his mouth. All these on I-80 are being remodeled. Some big corporation, bought up the contracts, gonna be arcades and showers and computer rooms, all sorts of stuff.

Huh. The father looks at the sky. Looks like it's going to piss down. The storm grows higher, black, green and grey, murky like lake water. Is it goooinnngg to storm? The son asks.

Nah, the janitor says, we never get it that bad here.

The father and son walk toward the front of the building. The janitor drops his cigarette on the ground and crushes it out with his boot. Across the highway the lone Caterpillar pushes dirt across the lot. The janitor imagines the new place: Starbucks and little churches, floors so clean you can see the bottom of your shoes as you cross them. Instead of Pizza Hut voids they will have Sbarro's and vegetarian salad bar buffets.

The Mennonite elder climbs into the driver's side of a fifteen-passenger van. It rocks some. He settles. The van was painted beige originally, or its original color had worn off over the years. The advertisement of its previous purpose was scrubbed poorly from the van's side, block letters picked and scraped until they were unrecognizable, the ruins of words. The elder cranks down the window and takes off his hat, his beard ripples in the wind.

The woman with the colorful dress clenches the book in her hand so tight her knuckles grow light at their points. She passes the janitor and the father, who has set down his yapping boy and is lecturing about parking lot safety. Her eyes are not closed but her mouth still moves in small ways, the reverberation of prayer. She comes to the passenger door and the elder reaches across and pushes it open. They share a smile. She settles. They pull away.

Suddenly a Bronco with a loose muffler cuts them off speeding across the lot. The man coming undone, asking for help, cries wildly with a long open mouth behind the wheel. The windows are closed. No one can hear him. The father nabs his son up, who is walking at his side. The Bronco, the man inside still crying, slams on its brakes and swerves, barely missing them.

Are you fucking crazy?! The father yells as the Bronco squeals away, toward I-80. The father is angry and unsurprised, knowing something like that would happen, something like that is always happening. See?! What'd I say?!

He's naughty, the son says.

The janitor walks over from the picnic table holding his unused broom, the Mennonites roll out of their spot and idle past the father, who is shaken and cussing. The Bronco muffler blares as it accelerates onto the highway into the storm. They all watch him speed away. They wonder what he needed so badly and where he was going to find it. The ripped American flag flaps faster and faster on a pole in front of the building. Nervous birds laugh and swirl West, away from danger. The janitor scuffs inside. The van creaks away. The father holds his son, swearing as they walk toward their car.

Jesus and Peter are still strapped in the bed of the truck. Jesus is shirtless. His hair falls over his face, falls like a canopy over Peter's feet, like a dead willow, to be cut down. Peter's leg is exposed, his right hand holding his knee, the other clamped to his thigh. The look on his face is pained, he winces as if Jesus is pulling a shard of glass from between his toes.

The storm inhales in the sky.

IVA WAS A RIVER

There was always water,
a rainy season, and Iva
was a river. Slow motion
clip of dam breaking,

imminent muscle but
drop by drop. You'd see
the stones she threw
before they hit you. Wide

and rushing, springtime,
lush greens lapping at her.
Or slim and cool and never
the same twice. Those who

entered knew, just had
to remember it. She'd change
you, then eventually, slink
right back to the ocean.

IVA'S FOLLOWER COMES HOME

The dog is afraid
of water. Even
of empty hose

unraveling,
it's that bad.
Like me, seeing

a man walking
up the drive.
The potential.

Shadow comes
first, all shoulder,
sound of steps

in silent grass.
Called a shut in
for closing

the drapes
at dusk. But listen.
I don't want

to be touched.
Broken window
and he bled

on the way in.
Used a hose
in winter

to clean up and
the dog cowed
while he

made love back
in the house.
Love of self

love of mother
love of money
of life of bedsheets

loath of self
of life, mother,
money. Long

mental list on which
I and bedsheets
remained and my

body became
dormant. Able
to live on stores

of sex
I'd gathered
for this coldest

season. I close
the drapes against
his gaze and my

legs against every-
one else and it is
years later. I want

to say I am sorry.
Most crave
violent sex

after these kinds
of episodes.
I am told this

by a lover
whose words, all
words, are meant

as invitations.
I am a smashed
broken thumb,

he says, an invitation,
a beg to fix as if
to fix one is to fix

all and self and
like a puzzle, unbreak
the glass. He wants

to be able to slap
and be slapped and
think it's helping.

All I want to do
is run the water.
But the dog is afraid.

But it would drown
out the noiseless
footsteps I strain

for. But the dog
is what I have. But—
I brought all of this

home and being
wet is useless.

THE FIRST TIME

Where she came from, people'd talk
about others they didn't understand,

say they were *touched*. Iva came to know
what this meant. First grade.

In the wide gym crosslegged cross from
the boy she thought she might love—

it came, her touch. Hit her, really.
There wasn't a light and nothing sung.

She didn't speak to it or about it but
sat. Stilled. Her cheeks held it hot.

A smirk she'd see again and again,
familiar for the first time, her unversed

legs standing her up and the searing
heat of his touch lighting up the black jersey

seam of her pants. Now she was touched
and that was the beginning of it.

Her love for him crawled up inside her
and she vowed never to let it out.

THEN IT REALLY BEGAN

Her life wasn't
riddled with bad,

though there were
stories she could tell.

But then
her baby got sick

and she wanted
not to live. No

belts or razor blades
or bottles of pills.

Rather, a slow, sweet
rot—fruit too long

on the bush—from
the inside, where

she couldn't see
to control it.

Her husband put
his hand on her

and once his thumb
was deep in decay,

he pulled back
and that was that.

JOSHUA ZELESNICK

~

let's invite the monster, a heartache may follow
but it only hurts when it crawls out of the ache
and pounds, the idea of the monster is only
my idea of the monster and none of my ideas

are entirely my own, forever wishing and hoping
cannot change the realness of the image, for instance
when the soldiers came in, the monster let them
and they stayed, how long can a group stay in a place

that isn't theirs, they asked the monster for input
on a matter, so the monster gave some shoddy input and they
whisked the monster away to a dark place with long corridors
that led to a vanishing point, torch lights,   a vast plain

~

the enemy is a monster
is the basic idea
of practically every war
mythology, we invade

from the air so we don't see
the monster's face mounted, the wall
between heaven and hell, little
pouches to collect their breaths

a little shrine to collect
our thoughts for the last time again
I want to become a robot, I
don't want to become a robot, I am

~

what's in a name,   everything
the nazis called the jews vermin
the operator's feed is too grainy
choppy, a child or a chicken

terrorist, insurgent, no,
an opera singer, hear that voice
spreads disease requiring quarantine
as in banned from the state, fear-based

clocks that wind backwards to show us
again who we really are and will
surely recognize a meme
in the mirror, wrecking ball

PAUL HANSEN

THEY KNOCKED OUT THE LIGHTS

My pals and I used to take pellet guns into the pastures, out beyond the corn and soy and slashing, and standing in the middle of all that endlessness we'd steady our weapons and fire at the testicles of newborn bulls. We had the summer months for target practice. Then the ranch hands would come in the autumn and castrate the calves and we'd be back to shooting soda cans off fence posts. I was the runt of us. My marksmanship was lousy. My hair was translucently thin. I was never entirely accepted.

Gerald, Lazy-Eye and Fen were my friends. After I moved away, Fen, aged sixteen, evaporated his stomach lining by drinking racing fuel to get drunk, but when we were young, we played epic pretend. My friends were excellent shots. They could hit a dangling target from twenty yards out. We had a deer hunting kit that Fen had lifted from his father and in the fields we'd camo-paint our faces and take aim. After a direct hit the newborn would writhe and we'd clench tight our smiles, crouched low. Then Fen would cup his hands to his face and say: "Comrades, the kill has been confirmed."

I am no longer young. These days I'm twenty-seven and I hate myself. My brain is corn and soy and slashing. My skin is caked red and cracked, frequently bloodied. It's severe plaque psoriasis and it's bad, all of my skin. I'm filled constantly with thoughts of not wanting to be me, of wanting to be dead me, of wanting to be any person that's not me. In twelve hours I will be dead.

I will not die alone, though. I have one friend, Ronald Slobowski, a once acclaimed musician, well-regarded in the indie world. We have a death pact. Tonight at midnight he turns twenty-eight. We'll die while he's still twenty-seven.

"The number thing is ridiculous," I told him two weeks ago when we made the handshake pact.

"No, no, no," Slobowski said. "It *has* to be while I'm twenty-seven. And it's got to seem accidental."

"That's stupid and romantic," I told him. "This is it and it's all there will be."

Slobowski looked dead at me. "I hope you don't actually believe that."

The brief taste of fame ruined him. At seventeen years old he home-recorded a strikingly beautiful record, heavily reverberated, released it to the web. It made the underground rounds, the tastemakers claiming he'd, "captured the last moment of youth." He did the tours, Europe and USA. An appearance on Late Night. But that was a decade ago and every album he's released since has been dismissed.

As for me, I hate who I am. Every smile is a reminder that my skin is sick. No woman has touched me lovingly so I've long detested touch. A defense mechanism, maybe, but seeing people touch makes a pit of spiders in my stomach. Fuck PDA's. I will die a virgin.

My skin has been this way since I was a teenager. No topical ointments, steroid injections or holistic things have helped. I've gone dairy-free, gluten-free, vegan. I've practiced meditation, cross-legged and embarrassed on the floor, trying to transcend. I have sought the advice of new-agey websites.

I haven't seen Gerald or Lazy-Eye since the pasture days. Fen's racing fuel death made the papers. I didn't attend the funeral. I couldn't stand to be back in that place. Forgiveness isn't in me. They are the ones that made me this way.

I was thirteen years old. We were shirtless and free with our firearms, invincible. After our second summer together, when the ranch hands castrated and left us without targets, we became constantly underwhelmed. Without blood we were nothing. I remember the day in black and white, in sepia, in anything other than color. It was an October Saturday. The morning smelled of lawnmower exhaust and the air siren test lingered over Iowa, 9am every Saturday. The four of us made quietly to the pasture, abandoned our bikes at the end of gravel, walked the rest of the way. My friends kept kicking dirt, their heads to the ground. I sensed something awry but kept with them anyways. We were unarmed, though Gerald carried a Dopp Kit. We went out past the corn and soy and slashing, all the way to our pine ridge, a hidden place where we'd cleared the brush, dug a fire pit, felled trees for chairs. There were cardinals on branches. All I felt was Iowa.

"Why didn't we bring the guns?" I said.

Fen and Lazy-Eye looked at each other.

"Time's come," said Gerald, reaching into the Dopp Kit, pulling out a notepad, a scalpel, three bottles of hot sauce, each homemade by their folks.

"I don't know, guys," Lazy-Eye looked around. "Maybe we shouldn't be doing this."

"No," said Gerald. "We've talked about it too much. We're not pussies, are we?"

"Guys?" I said.

"Ritter," said Fen, "you are the pussiest person we know. Now lay down like you're doing a snow angel."

"Guys?" I said again, slowly lying down.

"For fuck's sake, Ritter. This is for your own good."

When I was spread-eagled on the dirt, Fen and Lazy-Eye stepped on my wrists, legs. I looked straight up. Clouds made pictures in the sky. The pine trees lost their color above me.

"What's this about?" I said.

"No," said Fen. "Quit being such a pussy."

"All quiet on the Western front!" said Gerald, holding the scalpel. "Surgery is about to begin."

Gerald scalpeled three incisions up my forearm, each a quarter inch long and deep enough to bleed. I thought about how my father and I had pasted plastic stars to my bedroom ceiling, hand in hand. I always dreamt an endless night above me. Lazy-Eye looked away, his feet unsteady against me. The cuts came quick and clean. Blood made dry rivers on my arm. *I am not unlike you*, I thought. Gerald took tweezers to the first wound, held it open. Fen uncapped the hot sauce, dipped an eye-dropper into the bottle and dripped it in the cut. I stared through the clouds and thought of god. The burn spread through my arm, up the veins, into my heart.

"I score it a seven!" said Gerald. "Look at his face. It's a seven, for sure." He leaned closer. "It's definitely a seven and maybe even an eight." He made tallies in his notepad, repeated the process twice more. By the time they packed up and left, I didn't feel much. I walked slowly to my bicycle and when I got home, I looked my pussy self over in the mirror and put on a long-sleeve tee. Every Saturday for the next month I got the hot sauce treatment, the 9am siren test always overhead. I did nothing to end it. If I proved I wasn't a pussy, they'd eventually accept me.

That was damn near fifteen years ago. Being ugly on the outside made me ugly on the inside and now no person wants to know all of me. I was never famous, not like Slobowski. I am twenty-seven and virginal. I used to dream of wild-haired girlfriends but too many people look at me with pity and when every grocery line is an electric chair, there's no point in dreaming about anything other than being someone else.

–

Slobowski owns our apartment. He bought it outright with his music money. It's on the third floor of a converted warehouse in the recently renewed part of downtown. Now prettier people are wearing fewer things and the sidewalks are made of brick. Things were better when it was weird men in mustard-stained tees.

Gerald, Lazy-Eye and Fen kept up the hot sauce treatment through the autumn. Every Saturday we went to the fields where I'd pin myself down and make pictures in the sky. The leaves went from green to gold to dead and my skin gradually started reacting. Crusts formed on my knuckles and elbows. At first it wasn't bad but then on Thanksgiving Day, mother roasting turkey and the TV parade, my skin erupted with plaques. Red scales like spider webs across my hands, arms, elbows and chest. My parents took me to the doctor. He had me strip to my underwear. Scabs crept vine-like across my chest. My mother said nothing. She just sat there and breathed deep, deeper, deepest.

It's too much stress, said the doctor. The incisions had been sharp, the scars hardly visible. Had he really looked he would've seen. "Young man," he said, "would you consider yourself to be a high strung individual?"

"High strung?" said Dad. "He's a kid that rides his bike a lot."

I wanted to tell them that yes, it feels like my heart is swollen. That sometimes I have to remind myself to breathe. That I am ashamed. I didn't have it in me to rat on my pals. I'd let them do what they did.

The doctor taught me a few breathing exercises, applied topical ointment, encouraged me to find the green grass in my head. The ointment made me smell like July asphalt and that was the first time I truly hated myself, thirteen years old.

My friends saw flesh-wrecked me, the monster they'd made, and way out in the pasture they buried the scalpel. They looked at me, nodded apologies and we went our separate ways. A few months later my folks took jobs in Des Moines. We moved to the city, where I dressed in turtlenecks and wished constantly for winter, when I'd be able to keep gloved my disgusting hands. I stuck to my bedroom, talked to no one. The Des Moines people were pretty but they never acknowledged me. *You need no one*, I convinced myself. *It's only you.*

At twenty-two I took to drinking myself stupid in the old man places. Constant intoxication eased me. The old-timers took me as a younger them and never mentioned my condition. I was sitting in my favorite place, a Monday night, this dusty bar of Busch Light pride, and that's when I first heard Slobowski's guitar, drenched in reverb and his voice was pure. The music made Christmas lights in my chest. I knew then that there was another person who understood. I turned my stool, faced him. He played a half hour to scattered applause. As he packed his equipment I went and complimented his set.

"Come on," he said. "There's barely anyone here."

"It blew me away," I said. "It really did." I reached out my hand, wanting him to see me as I am. His grip was firm. He did not recoil. He did not blink. With my crusted hand in his, he said, "I used to play in front of lots of people, you know, but now it's this shit."

I was hooked. Slobowski and I made fast friends. I went with him to every show, once a month. Carried gear, helped set up. Sometimes people would come up and remember who he was. That always made me grin. Mostly no one cared. After a few months of friendship, I moved in with him. And now, five years later, we are twelve hours from dying together.

It's been years since I've spoken to my folks. I'm so bitter I all but told them to fuck off. They saw me wither into this and they used to tell me, sweetie, you notice it more than anyone; it's not actually that bad.

"Okay," I always said.

But I was so ashamed.

These years of friendship have been the highlight of my life. Slobowski doesn't mind my skin. The first time he saw me shirtless he said, "I'm sorry, man. I'm really, really sorry. I didn't know it was this bad."

"It is," I said. "It really, really is." And I wanted to tell him all about it: the bulls, the pellets, the scalpel and sauce, but I just looked at him and said, "people were pretty lousy to me."

And that night as I went to bed, I couldn't stop weeping.

Sometimes I feel like such a joke.

I hate grocery stores and people holding hands and I've long entertained the thought of dying, though never with any zest. My self-disgust has been pretty continuous. There's no one moment I can point to as the one in which I was broken. It's just too many wasted days stacked inside me. So, two weeks ago, two weeks before Slobowski's twenty-eighth, when he came to me and said, "I am going to kill myself," I looked at him and said, "I've thought of that before."

"It's the way to go," he said. "And if it's while I'm still twenty-seven maybe they'll go through my albums and regret not liking me while I was around. People always love musicians who died in obscurity."

"But suicide?" I said. "You actually want to?"

"No," he said. "Well, yes, but it's got to seem accidental. These people, there's no telling what they'll think if they know it was suicide."

"I don't know," I said. I was onboard but needed to know he'd thought it through. "Isn't writing a note half the fun?"

"Nah," he said. "It's got to seem accidental."

And so it was decided. We'd celebrate ourselves to death the night before his twenty-eighth birthday.

Slobowski spent his last two weeks recording. I walked around and knocked into strangers, pretending it was accidental, wanting them to feel their flesh against mine, wanting someone to stop and say: *you are okay.*

It's our dying day and we've got pills and booze and party streamers from the ceiling. There's rum, vodka, opioids. A small arsenal. Twelve hours. Twelve apostles. Twelve days of this Christmas. Mother, I didn't want you to see me like this. When you last saw me your face went soft. I wanted to explain my shame, but could only go away.

Fourteen years of staying hidden and untouched and they're still there, the scars up my arms. Look hard enough and you'll see. Give me gutters and dumpsters in alleys, not the pretty things. I'm going to where there's no cattle or scalpels, to where it's only electric guitars.

The party streamers are strung and Slobowski has finished his final mixes. He printed the master CD, labeled it: *Bummer*. Then he came to me. "You know you don't have to do this. Your face is really pale right now. You don't have to do this if you don't want to."

"Yes," I said. "I do have to do this."

He nodded.

"Slobowski," I said, "I know this is lame and everyone always thinks it's what they'd say given my situation, but I want to get laid before I die."

"It's not all it's cracked up to be. It's a lot of bad breath and weird hairs."

"Don't care. I want to know for myself."

"Everybody pretends to care, man. Everybody always does."

"Please."

"Fine. Alright. But don't say I didn't warn you."

Fourteen years of wanting to peel off my skin, of wanting my muscle and flesh to taste the outside air.

Twelve hours.

I won't die untouched.

Slobowski took to the web, asked if I had a hair preference.

No, I told him. Blonde, ginger, brunette, I do not care.

He found her on the back pages. I asked to see a picture. He said it's better as a surprise.

I hate cattle and pellet guns and pastures. I wonder if Fen took flight when the racing fuel ate his stomach. We used to be invincible. Now that I know I'm going to die it's hard to recall the way it was.

Eleven hours now. We have the music. The drugs. Friendship.

Before she arrived I double-brushed my teeth, ran a comb through my thin hair. I looked myself over in the mirror. Red vines across my chest, crusty and up to the neck. *This is you*, I said to myself. *This is it.*

She knocked. I put on my long sleeve. Slobowski answered, paid her in cash. From the bathroom I heard him say: "You treat him the way he wants to be treated, okay?" Then he went to his room and I stepped into the hallway. There she was in Shirley Temple lipstick, a light in her smile that says the worst has yet to come. She watched as I walked to her. The foundation I'd applied to my hands ran with sweat. She wore a red sweater, low-top sneakers. She stood before me.

"I haven't done this before," I said.

"It's okay. I haven't either if that's what you want."

"Keep saying that."

"What's your name?" she said.

"Ritter. It's Ritter."

"Ritter . . . What do you want me to be like?"

"I want you to fuck me like you mean it."

She lifted off my shirt. Her jaw tightened when she saw my chest, but still, she touched.

"I'm sorry," I said.

"Don't say that. It's not so bad."

"Keep saying that," I said.

"It's not so bad. I've seen things that are worse. Do you want me to take off my sweater? Some guys like it if I leave it on."

I nodded and put my timid lips to hers.

With my mouth against hers, she undid my jeans. "I'll fuck you like I mean it," she said, sliding down my pants, underwear. I watched as she went to her knees. Then I watched her eyes sink, her pupils drift to a far off place. A place of white beaches and stonewashed houses and little Spanish kids running around. She took a deep breath and stood, her sweater still on.

"I'm sorry," she said, taking the cash from her handbag. "I'm

111

sorry but I can't do it."

"It's not contagious. I swear."

She put the cash in my hand, pressed my fingers around it, looked at me with the same pity they always have.

"Keep it," I said, pushing it back at her. She let it fall to the ground, walked away. I watched her the whole way out, my pants down and shirt off. Slobowski came from his room. "What happened?" He looked at the money.

I nodded toward my flaccid self, dead skin flaked across it. "Why'd she think it would cut off at the belt?"

Slobowski looked at me.

"Why?" I said.

Slobowski came close to me, looked at the ground. Then he took hold of me.

It's all hideous and I am ugly.

He gripped me gently and said, "It's not that bad."

Blood rushed my veins.

"It's not," I said.

Then he dropped to his knees, inhaled, exhaled, and took me in his mouth. I closed my eyes and tried to see fireworks.

Slobowski went all the way. Then he stood, looked at me.

"Thank you," I said.

And we went together to the kitchen.

"The best ones went down like this," he said, uncapping the pills. "They'll remember us."

We set forth to die on the wings of angels, swallowed, crushed, snorted.

Wherever I go next, I hope there are plastic stars on the ceiling.

"I hope I get to meet Kurt Cobain in heaven," said Slobowski.

I smiled. I want them to put plastic stars in my coffin. Even if they never light up, I'd like to know they're there.

"Slobowski," I said, fading. "I'm terrified."

"Me too. But it'll be alright."

One bottle of rum, ten pills in and we started on the vodka, nine hours till midnight.

"Is there anyone we should call?" I said.

"I don't know, but I don't think so."

"You know . . . thanks for doing that earlier."

"Let's not talk about that right now, man. Let's just be happy."

"No," I said. "Thank you."

"It's not that bad," said Slobowski.

Eight hours, the bottle of vodka, six more pills and my lungs folded. Slobowski looked at me and said, "I don't know if this is the right thing to do." His voice was quiet, his face hung with resignation.

I wasn't sure either. From that close, the end was terrifying. Darkness until the end of time and nothing to light the stars. It was too late. I fell to the floor. He followed. He touched his arm against mine.

"I've never been this afraid," he said.

I felt my body sink through the floor.

They made me this way.

May they all feel guilty until the end.

I touched Slobowski. He touched me.

I fell into drifting clouds, over the corn and soy and slashing.

I heard gentle electric guitars.

I dreamt I was a plastic star on someone beautiful's ceiling.

AUDRA PUCHALSKI

SAINT ALBAN OF MAINZ

I definitely do not want pain, so that's
established. So why do I always think
I do? I thought I couldn't be
a person until a man hurt my feelings
but he never did, hair flip.
A thick white ring of mold wrapped
around a terracotta pot with flowers
living in it. As if nothing's real but
intensity, as if life's not mostly filling
out forms and the same six songs over
and over, and tripping in the thicket
slicing up my legs on the garden roses'
long black thorns, thinking *there you are!*
at it, a half-second smug with virtue, then
the mist parts and I scramble to close
the curtain up again, *oh no not like that
I don't like that at all*. I don't even wanna
shiver, evenings without my jacket, triceps
twitching holding my body back
from the sensations as though they
were my yoga mat in plank but
instead of a mat a gravel road and
instead of plank, about to faceplant in gravel,
and my bones gravel from being crushed
—not by a man—the soft flesh fled or flayed
open and shattering exposed, radiant
and I am dazzled, licking the pebbles,
mist in my mouth and once again carrying my

leathering disembodied head to my grave
because I'm helpful like that. *Go ahead,*
I said, or *yes please, cut off my head,*
I have a weird feeling I'll kinda like it, I said,
stupid. Walking the labyrinth of the hillside,
carrying my own head and entering this
hillside in my index of the numerous hillsides
where I have carried my own head helpfully
to my grave, the nostrils flared with the sharp
intake of breath, the throat stretching open,
the labyrinth of passages inside the head
can be distracting if you're not sure where
you're headed and I'm not. Which way to my
grave today? Anatomy, index, leatherbound
books, folds in the brain, forget what I don't
want, sinuses, forget the location
of my grave, synapse, forget the rosebush tangled
in my path, uvula, forget the severe drudgery of
these verdant hillsides, drudgery especially
severe with the heavy depressing cargo
of my body and yeah when I think about it
my head too, the whole thing complaining
every step and nowhere to get rid of it.

SAINT LAWRENCE

"I'm well done on this side. Turn me over!"
— Saint Lawrence, martyr and patron saint of cooks and
comedians, whilst being tortured on a hot gridiron

I walk around, sharp object
in hand, unable to not imagine it
plunging into my abdomen—
a martyrdom. Or
I switch on the burner and see
my hand slammed down
on the hot coil, and a kind of
relief. I am the prefect
who tortures me

and I am the mom
who hassles tirelessly
the child of me: not to touch,
to hold the knife point down,
to pull up my tights.

So all winter
in Michigan,
I picked my way down
treacherous frozen sidewalks,
my wool tights
webbed slightly
beneath my crotch
like the toes of an amphibian
evolved for speed through water.

My skirt fell
around my thighs,
a veil to obscure
my deformity. At any moment
I was ready to swim

rapidly away,
to propel myself
down the Huron River
through Ypsilanti
and Flat Rock,
to the Detroit River,
down the length
of Lake Erie
and Lake Ontario,
to follow the St Lawrence River
into Lake St Lawrence
and more St Lawrence River,
down the Canal de Beauharnois
into Lac St Louis,
more St Lawrence River
and then Lac-Saint-Pierre,
more St Lawrence River
and then the Gulf of St Lawrence
and then the Atlantic
to live out my days roving
the oceans,
a great monstrous
humanoid woolfish
of the sea.

KATHERINE MacCUE

CASSANDRA CONTEMPLATES
ALL HALLOW'S EVE

It is Halloween, Cassandra is going
as Cassandra, no one believes her,

as in, voilà, *c'est exactement comme*
magique — watch me pull my thumb

off, watch me spin in my devil horn,
watch me eat blood-oranges,

quartered, spliced like a Sicilian
thumb, a deeper red dripping from

this knife I lick with my black tongue.
What decade, Cassandra, though,

himation white? Or go-go boot blue?
Cassandra leans on the edge

of a doorway frame, a cigarette hangs
from her mouth, the cherry smoke

illuminates words of wise heroes;
to fall directly forward as if the fire

lies within, to not go as the glass in
his eye but the shard. Cassandra is

deep in thought, caught mid-frame,
stubs out the cigarette, flicks it into

a potted plant, decides to stay in, watch
the birds walk. She sheds her silence

by dropping fistfuls of orange peels
through the window onto the street

as if to join the flock, join each fracture,
syllable of her name, brush the mass

Wisteria of hair, logically, take a shower
to peach-pink aster, as in Cherry Blossom

skulls, handfuls of forget-me-nots,
to press into my belly button a universe

of Cassandras. She wraps herself into
a red candle, waxes on in drip drop that

all beings out there find themselves,
beauty mark or lesion, slut of the Sistine

Chapel, or else fall asleep, as she does,
with dreams of kitsch-angels running wild

outside in scarlet frocks.

CASSANDRA'S THANKSGIVING

It is Thanksgiving, Cassandra's aunt
is watching her read a magnet on
the fridge: *dinner will be ready*

when the smoke alarm goes off.
Cassandra's mother calls her sister
witch, the burnt turkey casting sleep

on an entire household. The bags
under Cassandra's auntie's eyes blow
sad confetti, another trick! Zoo animals,

rhinoceros, giraffes, lions, woozing,
walking up and down the stairs in different
post-coital measures to an ebony

piano that plays Liszt all by itself,
cranked, though Cassandra's grandmother,
in a state of dementia, thinks it is

Matthias, an old boyfriend from Germany
who has come back to save her; she even
assumes a stronger German accent along with
the piano's, — *did I say save?*

I mean, serenade:

Oh, my Liebestraum, when you
play that song, it's as if you make
love to God, or you are, through God,
making love to me.

CASSANDRA'S CONFESSION

Even so, Cassandra will admit
she, despite his tart kiss,
ferocity to have her so wildly

it curdled into curse, despite that
ridiculous song he'd play on repeat

— *I Saw Red* —

Cassandra loved Apollo,
loves him still; that stupid discus
he held, holds, dreams of holding,

as his sinewy body leapt
spun, still, from clover leaf
to clover leaf landing steady

on the ground of Cassandra's
thoughts, at the hour of daydreams.
She is just baffled broken

by his brain: its inability to
grow past lust. Apollo,
so unlike a real man but oh so

like a god, how he smiles,
lifts his head and lets go.

CASSANDRA'S BEAUTY

Cassandra drips chandelier,
prowls the summer night in midriff,

yawns hummingbirds, scarab beetles, too.
She moves in romantic gesture

with the wind, stares *into* the mirror,
lifts the fossil of her face

with her index finger, rings of curls
spiral out like outdated telephone cords;

rare, relic, long distance call, the ocean's
offing point, a meandering trail.

Hello? How did a teardrop turn into
an axe, and why were tears deemed

so lovely in the vague prehistoric?
Cassandra has had her tears, thinks

of rats with no names. She sat outside
her stoop once, smoking Virginia Slims

as they scavenged garbage bins bookending
her body. Something dropped at her foot,

a clip for her hair; the rats found it,
gave it back, an act of recognition,

of synchronous oneness which provided,
for Cassandra, symmetry in a world

of smoke and spit. That night she wasn't
beautiful, or she was, if you believe this poem, that is.

CASSANDRA BEFORE SHE WALKS TO HER DEATH

Now that it's time.
Now that Nico hovers above
all *pale blue eyes* in threes
like a beautiful hallucination
of the fates —

Now that Agamemnon's screams
provoke a vision of her own beheading,

Cassandra suddenly becomes thoughtful,
considers what life was like

Before this bloody end — (*après moi, le déluge*)

Before Apollo's kiss and spit of lemonseed

Before the rape at the hands of Ajax

Before she dressed her brother up
in blue eye shadow and blue silk
and he said it felt right and she said, *I know*

Before she and Electra took to
the swings listening to
Mariah Carey's "Greatest Hits"

Before the day she and Helen painted
their back legs, thighs, bottoms in
sacred pig's blood and from the mirror

looking over their shoulder their lower
halves appeared as devil wings blooming
up and up ready to spread and kiss the air

Before Cassandra cut her wrist amidst
the slaves scything in the fields

Before Cassandra read *Ulysses*
in bed telling her parents she
was sick with a cough

Before she rejoiced in Joyce, when
he said, *smackwarm.*

What was life like?

Life was not warm family by
the hearth. It was cold art; mostly
dinners at the Ivy, the drone of

the Hiltons' in a close corner,
a thin elbow resting on a balcony,
press-on nude lipstick, shoplifting

at Bijan, wearing nothing but
a one-thousand-dollar tie and musk.

Frankly, life was all look but don't touch.

Sure, so much free bottle
service à la table, so many dead

bodies to tip-
        toe
    over.

THE GATEKEEPERS

Janet and Blair were only inches from the supermarket exit when Blair gasped and announced she had to double back for, of all things, a packet of vegan cheese substitute. She had been gone for all of three minutes, leaving Janet to watch over their purchases, when who should breeze through the sliding-glass doors but Stephanie fucking Simmons in exercise pants. Janet's heart lurched at the sight of her old friend, the very person she'd hoped to avoid an hour earlier as she hustled Blair out of the house for this errand, knowing full well her chances were low: In more than twenty years as neighbors, and especially in the decade since their nests had emptied, Janet and Stephanie had done their shopping with unplanned but near-perfect synchronicity. Chances of Janet's *not* running into Stephanie on a Saturday morning were close to nil, hard as she'd hoped otherwise.

"Hello!" said Stephanie, pushing her shades up the slope of her forehead. She had a basket over one elbow and the unhurried look of someone embarking on a casual, just-a-few-things-I've-run-out-of sort of grocery trip, because why shouldn't she? Christmas was a whole three weeks off; only a total fool would already be out buying the makings of elaborate holiday cooking. Only an idiot who'd let herself be bullied into playing second fiddle to someone else's late-December travel plans.

"Hi, honey," said Janet, receiving the cheek-peck Stephanie offered her. She tried to use her body to obscure the segregated contents of her shopping cart: Blair's canvas bags of fresh produce at one end, her own processed and dairy foods in paper bags at the other, a plump wrapped turkey playing sentry between them. Of course, it didn't work; Stephanie seemed to be looking right past her, directly into the cart, taking inventory. "Just grabbing a couple of things," added Janet anyway. "You coming from spin class?" Immediately, she regretted prolonging the conversation; somewhere behind her back, Blair was probably halfway through the express lane by now.

"I quit last week," said Stephanie. "That teacher was like a barking chihuahua. Got on my damn nerves. I've started running in the neighborhood, though! Once, as of today." She laughed and loosed her hair from its high post-workout ponytail. It fell in smooth waves around her shoulders, freshly pressed and colored, not even a hint of silver at the roots. There had been some question about whether she could pull off chestnut highlights with her in-between skin tone, but overall it worked, the whole effect working in a later-career Pam Grier sort of way.

At a better time, and in a better mood, Janet might have brought forth a compliment. Now, though, from somewhere nearby came Blair's voice floating out above the noise of the aisles, a crystalline contralto loudly declining a bag. "Well, good for you," said Janet to Stephanie, desperately, and moved to give the cart a suggestive little push. "I'll see you —"

But then here were a hand on her arm and a *whoosh* of citrus-scented air to herald Blair's return; as Stephanie watched, her coiffed head tilted ever-so-slightly to one side, Blair dropped the Daiya Mozza into the open mouth of a canvas bag and her wallet into the empty child seat of the grocery cart. "Found it!" she said to Janet; and then, to Stephanie, "Hi!"

Earlier in the week, there had been an incident at the university, reports of a student protest turning violent, necessitating shelter-in-place tactics in Janet's building and the ones adjacent. It had happened at five minutes to three, just before Janet's scheduled appointment with a student wanting to raise hell because of his various grievances with Janet's teaching style and late-work policies. The sort of young man who, like so many of them did these days, felt that the problem with his grades reflected the faculty's failures to tailor the fabric of the university — of academia itself — to *him*. Janet had dreaded the meeting for days, had spent the hours of this particular day praying God would send an ice storm or something like it through the city to spare her of yet another of these conversations with yet another of these entitled kids; and then, with five minutes to go: the shelter-in-place mandate. A well-timed miracle that had apparently gotten the best of the student's pervasive laziness; even after the lockdown had lifted, the threat defused by 3:05, the kid had simply emailed a two-word discouraged cancellation: *Never mind*.

Was it too much to hope that something like that might happen now? Not an act of violence or a natural disaster, necessarily; but — surely God's imagination was better than Janet's — some unexpected escape valve to spare Janet from having to reintroduce her curious neighbor to her out-of-town guest. Stephanie and her constant hurry, her cell phone that never seemed to stop buzzing — where was the sudden urgent call?

But it seemed that Janet's luck for the week had run out. "Hello!" returned Stephanie. She turned her big berry-colored smile on Blair and then back on Janet, pushed a hand through her chestnut waves. "You have a shopping buddy."

"I do. You remember Blair, my —" started Janet, and faltered. It was like searching a drawer for a lost object in the dark; her mind's fingertips grazed various options — *son's girlfriend, granddaughter's mother* — but, with the one they really wanted not there, couldn't do much other than push this clutter aside. The moment stretched and yawned wide open.

"I'm William's partner," said Blair. She offered Stephanie her hand, bitten-down fingernails and all. "You're Janet's neighbor, right? The other *gatekeeper*. We met before — must have been a few years ago, when William and I were last out here?"

"That's right," said Stephanie, her smile brightening with recognition. She took the younger woman's hand in her manicured one and gave it one firm little pump. "I *thought* I saw Will's car pull in this morning. Of course we've met before. How's that baby of yours? I was wondering when you'd bring her back for a visit."

Blair laughed. "Caswell is fantastic. Just awesome. And *so* not a baby. *Kindergarten*, can you believe it? Her daddy took her to the aquarium today so Janet and I could get some cooking done."

"Some serious cooking, it looks like."

"Ha! Right. We're calling it our Casual Not-Quite-Vegan Christmas Before Christmas dinner."

"*They're* calling it that," cut in Janet, startling herself. The other women looked her way, a little glint in Stephanie's eye suggesting she'd caught the bitter edge in Janet's words. Janet straightened herself, adjusted the strap of her purse. "Because, you know. December ninth isn't *really* Christmas."

Blair rolled her eyes skyward and gave an exaggerated little sigh. "*December ninth isn't Christmas*," she echoed mechanically, around a laugh. To Stephanie: "We'll be in Paris for Christmas itself." She reached into the cart and began plucking out canvas bags, hauling them one by one over her solid shoulders. Her fingers were deft, altogether avoiding the turkey and Janet's paper bags as though they posed a contamination risk; and when the Daiya Mozza packet slithered out onto the supermarket floor, she did a full-bodied arabesque to retrieve it. Tossed it with a flourish, letting it spin twice in the air before catching it in her upturned palm.

Stephanie stared, mystified. "Paris for Christmas," she repeated finally. "Isn't *that* a fancy trip for Miss Caswell. Do you have family there?"

"No literal family," said Blair. "But we'll crash with some very good friends of mine for the first few days. The rest of the time, we're at the mercy of some hotel that's barely in our price range. William's never been, and he was hard to convince, but I was determined! Do you know" — and here she leaned in, actually pressed a hand to Stephanie's wrist — "that he didn't even have a valid passport when we got together?"

A fist clenched, hard, in the pit of Janet's stomach. It was another of those moments that un-furled into an eternity, leaving Janet plenty of time to absorb its grotesque details: the fraudulent mozzarella on display in Blair's outstretched hand, the headless turkey spreadeagled in the cart, the millimeter-widening of Stephanie's eyes at Blair's theatrical disclosure. At least one and maybe both of Stephanie's children, Janet suddenly remembered, had studied abroad in college.

"Caswell's had hers since her second birthday," Blair went on.

"Well!" said Stephanie, and gave her mane another broad finger-comb. "You know, I'd better start shopping." She gave Janet a long look and then a small smile. "You ladies enjoy your cooking. Blair, it was so nice to see you again!"

On the way to Janet's Acura, Blair wanted refreshers on details she'd forgotten since Will's and her last visit years back. For how long had Janet and Stephanie known each other? What was it they had all chatted about together on Janet's lawn, Caswell still small enough to have slept through all the cooing, the stroke of Stephanie's admiring hand?

The fist in Janet's stomach made it difficult, but she managed answers. She told Blair — as they loaded the vegan groceries into the backseat of the car and the others into the trunk — that she'd moved into the house directly opposite Stephanie's when their children were still in grade school, their husbands still in the picture. They had playfully called themselves *the gatekeepers* because the channel between their homes was the only road into the cul-de-sac beyond, so that between them they could see nearly all the neighborhood comings and goings — each other's especially. It was a phone call from Stephanie, in fact, that had tipped Janet off to Will's first and last episode of high-school truancy; and Janet who had warned Stephanie when she spotted loose shingles to be addressed on the other woman's rooftop. From the two-decade tapestry of facts, Janet found a few threads to share; and then she shut the trunk with a bang. In the car, it for some reason took her three tries to insert the key fully into the ignition.

"Good God," murmured Blair after a time, as Janet steered the Acura through the parking lot and out onto the main street. "I couldn't stand to live under that kind of constant neighborly surveillance. I think you've just named the reason William and I won't be moving out to the suburbs anytime soon."

After that it was silent, blessedly so, until the drive was nearly over. Turning onto the street at the end of which Janet's cul-de-sac lay nestled, they passed — for the second time that morning — the corner playground where a dozen young families ran and climbed and laughed, not a soul among them yet in mind of Christmas.

"They could've skipped the aquarium thing altogether," Blair said brightly, for the second time that morning. "Cas would have been just as happy on that playground."

But of course it had been Blair herself to shoot down this very idea, presented hours earlier by Janet, seconded hopefully by a Will still exhausted from the road trip into town. The aquarium was nearly an hour's drive away; the playground, within sneezing distance of Janet's front door. Regardless, Blair had practically shoved them down the driveway toward Will's car, peppering her goodbyes with unending instructions. *William, don't forget her snacks. Check the ingredients first if you're going to buy anything from the cafeteria. William, her coat isn't zipped all the way up. Nothing from the gift shop, William.* And then finally, as Will fiddled with the carseat, she'd turned momentarily sunny, waved her arms over her head to get Caswell's attention. *Hey Cas,* she'd called out. *Seeya, kid! Wang chung! Enjoy the fishies!*

Janet had watched from the doorway, the exchange stirring in her the uneasiness that would settle in and stay with her through the rest of Christmas Before Christmas. *Wang Chung.* She knew Blair had spent most of her twenties in Beijing, teaching English to native Mandarin speakers, and early on there had been ambitious talk of raising Caswell bilingual — maybe this was that? Caswell, seeming to understand, had thrown back a graceless wave of her own, her solid little torso vibrating with anticipation. Blair had her carrying her own things in a backpack, one almost half her body's size; she'd nearly dropped the damn thing, hopping and waving.

Wang chung. Janet had cast her eyes up to the façade of the

house across the street, not seeing Stephanie behind any of its great windows; grateful that even if she was watching from somewhere over there, she could hear none of it. Could only see Will — lanky, clean-shaven Will — helping into the car a child whose looks and build were nothing like his. Pushing aside her wild feathers of uncombed hair so he didn't accidentally trap them in the carseat buckles.

"Well, no one who knows better bothers with the Eiffel Tower," Blair was saying, sending a sweet potato across the gleaming blade of a mandoline. "Definitely not at Christmastime. It's a cesspool and a tourist trap."

"Oh," said Janet. She had lost track of how many spoonfuls of flour she'd yet stirred into the roux thickening on the stovetop. To be on the safe side, she added two more, then another splash of milk, and resumed her quick-wristed whisking. "Well, that's news to me. Will's father and I loved it. But that was back in the eighties."

Blair pulled a brand-new casserole dish out of a canvas bag and sat it on the counter, began laying slices of sweet potato across the bottom without rinsing it first. "There are other spots to see the city from," she said. "We'll go to Montmartre and climb the hill, or maybe do the Montparnasse observation deck if Cas is interested, and then she and Will can at least look *at* the Eiffel Tower."

"*If she's interested*," repeated Janet. "How would she know if she's interested?"

Blair reached back into her bag, frowning, and produced a can of organic tomato paste. "How would she know if she's interested?"

"She's a little kid, and she's never been to Paris. How would she know — well, why wouldn't you just take her there, if *you* think she should see it?"

Janet thought Blair gave a little snort; but maybe it was just a bubble in the tomato paste, an unappetizing little fart escaping as she layered it, viscous and red, across the mat of raw sweet potatoes. "She's five, she's human, she has opinions. We're not in the business of forcing her into experiences she doesn't want."

"Well, all right," said Janet. She took the roux off the burner and poured in the hand-shredded gruyere, overturned the bag of sharp cheddar on top of that.

Blair went on: "She enjoys the experience more fully, anyway, if she chose it herself. If it's something she really wanted to do."

Janet gave the cheese a good mix, covering the shreds with sauce, and let the spoon fall hard into the bowl. "All right," she said again, and turned to head out to the garage. "Getting some butter," she added, pointing.

There *were* a few extra sticks in the outdoor refrigerator, and Janet *would* need one of them to finish off the crumble dish she'd prepared the night before, Will's favorite; but mostly what she needed was a few moments of brisk December air. Outside, she shut the house door behind her and hit the button to send the garage door rolling to the ceiling. Fingers of cold slipped in and curled around her face. She thought of the student, the one who'd canceled that week, and what he'd written in one of his bit-ter emails: *My parents aren't paying this school for you to tell me I'm wrong about everything.* Which had baffled her, really; because — his inflammatory characterization aside — wasn't that essentially *exactly* what they were paying for?

Across the street, Stephanie's car was pulling in, her morning shopping and whatever other errands completed. Janet watched as the other woman climbed out of the driver's seat, pulled her hair carefully up into its protective knot, and began unloading items: her leather purse, her shopping bags, a weighty rectangular object wrapped in tape and brown paper. A family portrait, Janet remembered; one of the fancy posed ones — evidently back from professional framing. Stephanie had paid for the shoot, of course, but to their credit her children had cooperated; and it had turned out well, everybody smiling and wearing something that looked all right, though not the matching cabled sweaters Stephanie had first requested. Janet supposed Stephanie would hang it before the children came for Normal Christmas, all those days from now.

She wondered, with a start, whether Stephanie could see the makings of Blair's *sweet-potato lasagna*, as she'd called that mess in the casserole dish, or the many kitchen implements Blair had insisted on bringing from home or purchasing new at the grocery store, in perfect duplication with the contents of Janet's well-stocked cabinets? But, no. Both kitchens, Janet's and Stephanie's, faced the homes' respective backyards; only later, when the finished foods were carried out to the dining room, Will and Caswell assembled around Janet's dressed-up walnut table, might Stephanie catch a piece of Nearly Vegan and Whatever-the-Hell-Else Christmas Before Christmas. Caswell in her jeggings because why should a little kid be forced into fancy clothes to spend time with family? So Blair had said.

With a sigh, Janet hit the button to close the garage door and let herself back into the kitchen.

"I'll use the upper and you use the lower?" asked Blair, gesturing to indicate the ovens.

"Whichever," said Janet. She washed her hands, found her post, began pouring cooked macaroni into the integrated cheese sauce.

"Great," said Blair, and began jabbing at the row of buttons up top. "I cleaned the upper one out a little bit."

Janet checked the oven clock: noon, or very nearly so. "I'm opening some wine," she announced. On her way to the basement, she issued a command — *Jazz, please* — to the automated speaker Will had sent her last Christmas, silencing the faint strains of what Blair had called *new-wave British pop*. The friendly computer chose a bebop station playing Christmas staples; Janet nodded in moderate satisfaction. Enough of standing on opposite ends of the kitchen like they had sticks up their rears.

In the basement, she chose a cabernet franc that she liked very much and figured wouldn't suffer from lack of breathing time. Back upstairs — and now it *was* noon — she made a beeline for her glass with the little cluster of gold flecks along the stem, a gift from Will on some past Mother's Day, the only one like it in the house. She had the corkscrew in hand, inches from the bottle, when she remem-bered.

"Blair?" she said. "Can I pour you a glass?"

Blair looked over, her hands full of Daiya Mozza. "I'll take one," she said quickly. "Please."

The wine, and the buoyant Christmas music, helped considerably; finally, time moved like it had someplace to go. Blair moved on to start her Brussels sprouts dish at the stovetop; Janet gave the turkey its final lemon-herb bath and started the crockpot. The macaroni, bubbling in the lower oven, filled the room with the playful aromas of nutmeg and sharp cheeses.

"Hope they're having fun," said Blair after a time. "Caswell couldn't wait to see fishies."

"Will's father and I used to take him," said Janet. "They had those eels in the tank on the floor, that kids could touch — not sure if they do that anymore — and he went *bananas* over those eels. He loved them. But then there was the room where one whole wall was a shark tank — the sharks with all those teeth, like you would see in cartoons — and he went bananas over that, too, but in a bad way. He was sure one of those sharks was going to swim right through the glass and have a little-boy snack." She took a sip of her wine and closed her eyes, remembering: Will with his back pressed up against his daddy's legs, pearlescent little tears in the corners of his big cocoa eyes.

"Wow," said Blair.

"He got used to them later," added Janet, thinking of an older Will striding toward the tank on longer, more confident legs. "He probably doesn't even remember how scared he was at first."

"He was terrified of the sharks," said Blair slowly. "But you took him back to the aquarium anyway?"

Janet, topping off Blair's glass and then her own, didn't answer. It seemed like a question undeserving of a response; over the years, there had of course been countless invitations to the aquarium — from the Boy Scouts, the church youth group, the other university professors with kids around Will's age. Even considering all the times they'd declined — Will's homework or sporting events or playdates getting in the way — there must still have been dozens of visits, most of them overall positive. Delightful, even. Out loud, she said, "Pardon my reach," and knelt by Blair's waist to check the progress of the dishes in the lower oven.

"Why didn't he go with you, to Paris?" asked Blair from above. "When you went with your husband in the eighties."

Janet took her time in checking the dishes, testing the springiness of the macaroni with a careful finger. When she straightened up, she took another swallow of wine before answering. "That was before Will was born," she said finally, and set down her glass to begin the work of gathering up the dirtied dishes, the no-longer needed ingredients. "We went for our first anniversary. It was my husband's favorite city."

"But then you never took William?"

With her back to the other woman, Janet flung open a cabinet and returned the salt, the pepper, both types of paprika to the spice rack. "There wasn't a chance, after that," she said. "Will came, and then we spent the next twenty years on Will." She added, charitably, "You know how it is when they're little."

Although, Caswell's clothes and hair looking as they had that morning, maybe Blair *didn't* know; maybe she'd be shocked to know some people invested hours each week even on basic child-grooming rituals so the neighbors and the schoolteachers wouldn't talk. Will's father had faithfully broken out the clippers at seven-day intervals to shape the fleece at Will's nape and temples, a process involving much squirming, endless distractions, cajoling that turned gentler or firmer depending on how the child cooperated. All in the name of sending him out into the world each day with the look of a kid you might ask to join your debate team, and not one you'd worry would break into your car. Caswell, as far as Janet could tell, hadn't seen a comb since her last visit years ago.

She had reached the bottom of her glass again. "When you're

done with the stovetop," she said, pouring herself a refill, "I need to finish Will's crumble."

"Mm," said Blair, giving the skillet a little shake.

"Take your time," added Janet. "I'll go make sure all the beds are ready." Sidestepping the stovetop area, its woodsy smells of sprouts and balsamic, she took her wineglass and headed for the stairs that led to the second floor.

She'd put Will and Blair in the guest bedroom, Caswell in Will's old room. In the latter, Caswell's things lay scattered across the carpet: the toys that had occupied her on the long car trip, the garments she'd tried on and rejected before the aquarium. Janet set her wineglass on Will's dresser and started folding. Surely there was a theory at work—that children should control their own environments, or that a tidy room mattered less than Caswell's free exercise of sartorial choice—but a genera-tion earlier, a different theory had reigned over this same bedroom; and the result had been a child who'd kept his surroundings as meticulously neat as though he'd been paid to keep them that way. Whose teachers had praised him, highly and often, for the state of his cubby, his workspace, his physical person.

Janet's student, the complainer, had come to class twice that semester in low-hanging sweatpants and what she'd been sure was an undershirt, his dark-blond underarm fuzz caked with crumbs of deodorant. *THAT*, she'd have told Will, were he there to tell, *is what we couldn't have from you*. Thinking of the idlers who loitered just off-campus dressed exactly that same way, who could have been Will but weren't Will, no parents to insist they stayed in school, kept their hair cut close.

Even in neater piles, Caswell's clothes looked ratty and smelled well-traveled under the residue of her mother's tart handmade soaps. Involuntarily, Janet cast a look through what had once been Will's window, across the street and into what had once been the Simmons boy's. Some ten years ago, Stephanie had all but turned the room into a home gym; before that, though, it had been a hurricane of posters and unwashed laundry, the other

139

boy lacking in Will's careful fastidiousness.

But—Janet took a sip of wine, remembering—it had been a conscious decision of Stephanie's, letting that slide. You had to pick your battles with children. Stephanie's son, her baby, had given his parents fits for years, the daily struggle sending shoots of silver through Stephanie's hair long before her fortieth birthday. If Will had tried his hand at truancy once, the Simmon's boy's failed attempts had been downright chronic for a while; Janet had lost count of the number of times she'd seen his beleaguered parents stand watching in the morning as he descended the front steps and shuffled his way onto a school bus. Neither of them heading back into the house until the bus was all the way down the street, rounding the corner to, they fervently hoped, actually deliver him to school. That the child had earned his diploma on time, had matriculated to college, a good college, would be called a *miracle* if it hadn't involved years and years of backbreaking hard work. A full-time job for two. And if the Simmons boy hadn't ever learned to pick up after himself—well. He hadn't landed himself in jail, either. On the morning of one of his graduations, Janet had taken care to high-five his mother on her lawn, just as they'd done over Will's a few years earlier.

Wang chung. Each year, the school had sent its eighth-grade class to France at the culmination of its multiculturalism unit, two hundred burgeoning teenagers under the care of a handful of chaperones hardly a few years older. First Janet and then Stephanie had summarily declined to submit permission slips on their sons' behalves, Janet kept awake by nightmares of Will's being mistaken for a Parisian gypsy and locked in some juvenile-detention center an entire ocean away. It was the sort of thing that happened constantly, brown people the world over answering for each other's crimes; and earlier that same year, she and Will's father had endured a bitter battle with the school over Will's suspension just for standing *near* a fistfight on the basketball court. Gentle, cautious Will! Forgive her if she hadn't entrusted his international well-being to the same clutch of perky teachers who'd allowed *that* to happen. Anyway, he did model U.N. on Tuesdays after school, met with a language tutor on weekends. Not the same as seeing the Musée d'Orsay up close, maybe, but certainly safer.

She and Will's father had withstood their son's begging and brief indignant outburst, the short-lived hunger strike that followed, his embarrassed tears; when he'd had to do a little bit of supplementary homework to make up for what he'd missed in France, Janet herself had gathered the needed library books and coached him through it, rewarding his patience with Bullets tickets.

So they hadn't gotten around to taking him back over there. Even without leaving the continent, they'd turned out a great kid, both feet on the ground, unimpeachable manners, respect for his elders. He had shown affection freely to his parents and grandparents, offering hugs without being asked, none of the false shyness Caswell had shown at her arrival this weekend.

But Blair had been all over. To Beijing, to London, to Paris — enough times, apparently, to consider herself among those who would know better than to bother with the Eiffel Tower. And to Reykjavik, her ancestral homeland on one parent's side, where she'd been dazzled by the turquoise fjords she must have mentioned a dozen times at Janet's and her first meeting.

You've never heard someone use the word fjord *so many times in one sitting,* Janet would have said to Stephanie afterward, had she felt like talking about it.

She smoothed down the sheets encasing Will's old twin bed, pulling hard at the corners to get them crisp. His old Afrikids pillowcase was deeply wrinkled; she gave it a tug and then a punch, squarely to the middle. That helped, actually, so she did it again.

Several punches later, Will's pillow beaten into submission, she descended the stairs, wineglass in hand. Her cheeks flushed with exertion, and emboldened by the wine, she thought she might find it in herself to say something about the state of Caswell's borrowed room; at the very least, she could ask for compliance with the house rules. Kids cleaned up after themselves here, whether or not it was what they *wanted to do*.

But of course, Will already knew that, just as he'd known the corner playground was a perfectly fine place to pass a morning; that five-year-olds didn't get to set their own travel itineraries; that a little girl should have a little girl's name, rather than some fanciful unisex creation of her mother's; and that a little girl also deserved a single-family home in the suburbs, parents who cared enough to marry each other, all the things he and the Simmons children had had at costs he — and Blair — could barely imagine.

By the time she reached the bottom of the stairs, her wineglass empty, she knew she wouldn't say anything about the clothes after all. The visit was scheduled to last only two days, and there probably wouldn't be another for a while. Caswell would be a completely different child by the next one. Maybe the children in Montparnasse would have taught her to pick up after herself.

"They'll be here at three," said Blair, holding up her phone.

"Wonderful," said Janet. "May I use the stovetop yet?"

"Um, sure," said Blair, and removed the empty skillet from the front burner. "For the crumble you were talking about?"

"Just to brown the butter," said Janet, reaching for her smallest saucepan, the sticks still cold from the outside refrigerator. "There's not much else to it, after that."

"Okay," said Blair. She was quiet for a moment, refilling her canvas bags with the remnants of her groceries. Then she cleared her throat. "Well, what if you skipped the crumble?"

Janet frowned. "Why would I do that?"

"It's just that it's a lot to go through for something most of us won't eat. Too much butter for Caswell."

Janet's frown deepened. "But Will would want it." Will at twelve, shoveling seconds onto his plate; at twenty, road-tripping home from college for the holidays and hopefully sniffing the air for the scent of cinnamon the second he walked in, before even saying hello.

"Maybe not. He'll have turkey and some of your macaroni — he's been talking about it for days — but he's otherwise doing pretty well lately, staying the course."

"So he's vegan now."

Blair laughed, a little dryly. "Sort of. Lightly so, with coaching. He's the *casual, not-quite-vegan component* of Casual Not-Quite-Vegan Christmas Before Christmas."

Janet had pulled two half-sticks of butter out of the box; now she slid them back into the box, wordlessly returned her saucepan to the cabinet. "All right," she said after a moment. "No crumble."

Blair hesitated. "Maybe you could serve just the berries themselves with a little brown sugar," she said with forced brightness. "I know we'd love that!"

In her glittering turquoise eyes was a look Janet knew too well from her own maternal repertoire, the same practiced cheer she'd shone on Will to sell a Bullets game as a stand-in for the missed trip to France. "Maybe," she said lightly. "That's a good idea." She pinched shut the box of butter sticks with a chilled thumb and forefinger. Then: "Blair," she said, just as lightly.

"Yeah?"

The fist in the pit of her stomach had unclenched itself, its fingers unwinding themselves up toward her throat. "I'm getting tired," she croaked, shaping the words into an apology, a guilty admission. She held out the box of butter. "Would you take this to the garage and put it back into the outside fridge? Since we're not using it after all?"

"Sure!" said Blair, taking the box, visibly lighter after the success of the negotiation.

"And while you're out there," added Janet, her voice tight around the fingers in her throat, "we need the leaf for the dining-room table."

"For just the four of us?"

Janet managed a nod and a smile. "All the food. The turkey and all the casserole dishes, so we don't have to keep coming back into the kitchen."

"Okay. Where's the leaf?"

Janet described its location, indicating that Blair should check the wall behind her late husband's old Mercedes. "It's propped up on its side. Be careful over there."

"Okay," said Blair, and spun on her heel. She let herself out into the garage; Janet heard the door to the outdoor refrigerator open and then quickly close.

She turned her attention back to the state of the kitchen. Blair had reclaimed all her personal dishes and put away some of the others, had shoved the cork back into the half-full wine bottle. Janet lifted the bottle and gave it a swirl, watching the ruby-colored liquid dance behind the glass. On the granite countertop, Blair's wineglass sat nearly full. Janet wondered whether she'd had better in Montparnasse.

After a time, Blair came back into the kitchen, carrying the wooden leaf under one arm. "Found it," she said, quietly.

"Great. If you put it in the dining room, we can let Will put it in when he gets home."

Blair started for the dining room, then stopped at the doorway. "You keep a crib in your garage?" she asked lightly, over one shoulder.

Janet managed a frown. "A crib . . . ?"

"There's one behind that other car in the garage."

"Ah," said Janet, as if remembering.

"It must not be William's. It looks new. Just dusty."

"No," said Janet. "We gave his away decades ago."

"So what's that one for?"

Janet gave an ambiguous little gesture: half shrug, half dismissive wave. "There was a sale at a baby store going out of business," she said vaguely. "It was five or six years ago. Stephanie Simmons across the street and I both impulse-bought them, thinking we might need them for grandchildren who'd be around a lot." She paused and reached for a carton of berries, began rinsing them in preparation for their changed destiny. "You learn to adjust," she said, almost to the berries.

Blair's pale eyes darkened. The arithmetic needed was quick; *five or six years ago* put the purchase just before Caswell's birth. "Oh," she said, and kept walking.

When Janet finished rinsing the berries, it was five minutes to three; punctual Will, rarely a minute later than he said he'd be, would have already turned off the highway by now. She walked into the foyer and looked out at Stephanie Simmons's house, trying to locate her neighbor behind one of its many windows. There was movement west of the front door, in the playroom-turned-TV room, where Stephanie sometimes fell asleep on the same couch on which Janet had once seen the Simmons daughter climbing on top of the no-good boy they'd spent the next two years prying her off of.

That made Janet chuckle, remembering that, but only because she knew how it had turned out: They'd rid the daughter of that particular boy and fended off similar threats for long enough to see the daughter through the rest of her fast-assed adolescence. She'd made it to medical school, married a nice man, had babies — unlike Janet, Stephanie *did* have occasional reasons to use the crib she'd bought at the sale those years back.

Behind her, Janet heard Blair ascend the stairs, calling out that she wanted to change out of her cooking clothes. There were five minutes, maybe more if Will happened to hit a snag in the neighborhood traffic. Janet saw that Stephanie was watching a home-shopping show, the sort of idle programming she'd have on in the background while doing her laundry. Janet wondered whether she'd like to split the last of the cabernet franc, whether they could polish it off in the five-or-more minutes it might take Will and Caswell to make it home for dinner.

She let herself out the front door and was hit with another memory: Last Christmas, Normal Christmas, on her way out to dinner with friends, Janet had watched the Simmons boy — a man now, slighter than Will and more sharply dressed — climb Stephanie's front steps with his hand laced through the hand of another young man. Janet had watched them share a kiss under

Stephanie's mistletoe-adorned porch light, their lips and hands parting just before the front door opened.

There was something she had always wondered. If Stephanie had been home at the time of Janet's and Blair's surprise first meeting, then maybe she had spied something similar in the moments just before Janet answered the doorbell? Maybe she had watched Will and Blair hold hands up the walkway, watched them kiss on the porch, watched Will stare adoringly into Blair's fjord-colored eyes as they waited to be let inside. Maybe Stephanie had noted Blair's eclectic maternity hand-me-down frock—had known, for seconds or minutes before Janet had, about the coming baby that was to be Caswell. But just as Janet hadn't said boo about the Simmons boy, then or afterward, Stephanie hadn't breathed a word about Will's new family, either. Hadn't asked till she'd been told. Which was a funny thing to think about, really.

Janet thought of Stephanie at the supermarket this morning, her hair freshly laid, her manner as relaxed as a woman's could be only when her children were off in their corners of Elsewhere, presumably doing exactly what they were supposed to be doing. What they'd been raised to do. But in years past, still in the throes of raising teenagers, still anticipating the loss of her husband to his persistent mistress, Stephanie had—rather regularly—appeared at the supermarket looking like a different person altogether, an angry and haggard person, an inch of silvery new growth at her temples.

Janet giggled at that—mentally overlaying the beaten-down Stephanie of certain past supermarket trips onto the carefree glory of this morning's Stephanie. Wasn't it a little funny that, two weeks or so from now, Normal Christmas descending upon them like an anvil, it would be the angry, haggard Stephanie—the one anxious about her children and in need of a touchup—out doing the shopping, while Janet relaxed and watched home shopping, Vegan Christmas blessedly behind her?

Janet's giggle bloomed into a bubbling laugh; by the time she reached the driveway opposite her own, she was laughing aloud to herself. Stephanie's front door opened several beats before Janet made it up the front steps; Stephanie, when she moved aside for Janet to enter and took the bottle from her hand, was laughing too. *"Caswell's had hers since her second birthday,"* mimicked Stephanie, just that; it was all she could manage before she lost her breath. They wasted at least two of the five minutes that way, both of them doubled over in the foyer, laughing without speaking, as Janet felt — firmly and suddenly — that they'd earned the right to do.

Contributors

EMILY ALEX is the fiction editor at Noemi Press and a fiction editor with *The Rupture*. She has an MFA from New Mexico State University and works for a literary agency in New York. Some of her work can be found in *The Offing*, *Full Stop*, *Heavy Feather Review*, *Denver Quarterly*, and *Tupelo Quarterly*.

NICHOLAS BON is the author of *My Circus Mouth* (Ghost City Press, 2018) and the editor of *Epigraph Magazine*. They live in Tallahassee, where they attend the MFA program at Florida State University, and can be found online at nicholasbon.com.

JENNIFER CONLON is from North Carolina and earned her MFA in poetry from Arizona State University. She was awarded the 2017 Katherine C. Turner prize from the Academy of American Poets. Her poems have been published by or are forthcoming in *Bayou Magazine*, *Bennington Review*, *DIALOGIST*, *Threadcount*, and elsewhere. Jennifer lives in Tempe, Arizona, where she teaches freshman composition.

REILLY D. COX is an MFA candidate at the University of Alabama in Tuscaloosa. They attended Washington College and the Bucknell Seminar for Younger Poets. They have work available or forthcoming in the *Academy of American Poets*, *Always Crashing*, *Tupelo Quarterly*, *Rougarou*, *Cigar City Journal*, *Adirondack Review*, *Cosmonauts Avenue*, *Rust + Moth*, *Foothill*, and others.

EVAN J. CUTTS is a 24-year-old Boston-native, poet, writer, and Chancellor's MFA Mentors Fellow at Rutgers University — Newark. Evan was a member of the Emerson College 2017 CUPSI Team and 2017 National Poetry Slam "Last

Chance Slam" Team. His poetry navigates Blackness, locality, mythology, and magic. His poetry is published or forthcoming in *LUMINA*, *Apogee Journal*, *Voicemail Poems*, *Maps for Teeth*, *The Merrimack Review*, *Jabberwock Review*, and *The Offing*.

BRIAN EVENSON is the author of more than a dozen books of fiction, most recently the story collection *Song for the Unraveling of the World*. He has been a finalist for the Shirley Jackson Award five times and has won the International Horror Guild Award. He has received Guggenheim Foundation Fellowship and an NEA Fellowship, and three of his stories have received O. Henry Awards. He teaches at CalArts and lives in Los Angeles.

MICHAEL A. FERRO'S debut novel, *TITLE 13*, was published by Harvard Square Editions and selected as a "Best Book of 2018" by the Emerging Writers Network. He was named as a finalist by *Glimmer Train* for their New Writers Award, won the Jim Cash Creative Writing Award for Fiction, and been nominated for the Pushcart Prize. Michael's writing has appeared in *Michigan Quarterly Review*, *Monkeybicycle*, *Poets & Writers*, *Heavy Feather Review*, *Vulture*, *Crack the Spine*, *Duende*, *BULL: Men's Fiction*, *Entropy*, *Splitsider*, and elsewhere. Born and bred in Detroit, Michael has lived, worked, and written throughout the Midwest; he currently resides in rural Ann Arbor, Michigan. Additional information can be found at: www.michaelaferro.com.

PAUL HANSEN lives in Tallahassee, FL. Other work has appeared in *Fanzine* and *New Ohio Review*. He is a Ph.D. student at Florida State.

JENNA LÊ (jennalewriting.com) authored *Six Rivers* (NYQ Books, 2011) and *A History of the Cetacean American Diaspora* (Indolent Books, 2018; 1st ed. Anchor & Plume, 2016), which won Second Place in the Elgin Awards. Her poetry appears and is forthcoming in *AGNI Online, Bellevue Literary Review, Denver Quarterly, Los Angeles Review, Massachusetts Review, Michigan Quarterly Review,* and *West Branch.*

ELLYN LICHVAR is the managing editor of *The Louisville Review.* She is also a coordinator for Spalding University's low-residency MFA in Writing Program. Her work has appeared or is forthcoming in *DIAGRAM, BOAAT, Meridian, Whiskey Island, The Journal, The Boiler,* and elsewhere.

DASCHIELLE LOUIS is a Haitian American poet, writer, and graphic artist from South Florida: her work uses magical realism to examine blackness, womanhood, Haitian culture and migration. Daschielle's poetry and short stories have appeared in spaces such as *Token Magazine, Linden Avenue Literary Journal, Moko Magazine, Panku Literary and Arts Magazine, Rise Up Review, Transition Magazine* at The Hutchins Center, *Vagabond City Lit,* and *Wusgood Magazine.* Her literary work is housed on her website daschiellelouis.com.

KATHERINE MACCUE is a poet who lives in in New York. She recently earned her MFA at Hunter College in NYC. Her first book of poems, *No Timid Electra,* came out in 2014. Her work has been published in various journals, including *decomP, Word Riot,* and *Vinyl,* and she has been nominated for the Pushcart Prize four times. She is currently working on her second book of poems.

When she isn't writing, **CHRISTINE MA-KELLAMS** teaches at the San Jose State University. Her fiction has appeared in *ZYZZYVA, Kenyon Review, Baltimore Review,* and elsewhere.

JENN MARIE NUNES is the author of *AND/OR* (2015), winner of the Switchback Books Queer Voices award, and seven chapbooks, including *Juned*, winner of the YesYes Books 2015 Vinyl 45 Chapbook Contest, and the collaborative *HYMN: An Ovulation* (Bloof Books, 2015). Her work appears in numerous journals, including *ACTION, YES!, Ninth Letter, Black Warrior Review, DREGINALD, [PANK],* and *smoking glue gun,* and she is co-founding editor of *TENDE RLOIN,* an online gallery for poetry. Her second full-length collection was selected as the winner of the 2016 National Poetry Review Press Book Prize and is forthcoming. Jenn is currently pursuing a PhD in Chinese Language and Literature at OSU.

AUDRA PUCHALSKI lives in Oakland, California. Her work is also published or forthcoming in *The Collagist, Cosmonauts Avenue,* and *Bat City Review,* among others.

SHANNON SANDERS is a Washington, DC-area attorney and test-prep instructor. Her fiction has appeared in *SLICE* and *Requited Journal* and was featured in *Puerto del Sol*'s Black Voices Series.

STELLA SANTAMARÍA is a Latina Poet who grew up in Miami. Stella believes that poetry should not be restricted only to paper or on a screen, but heard, sung, chanted, rapped, and performed. Santamaría thinks poetry is a forum where the world can be changed one space or letter at a time. Her poetry has been published in *Pennsylvania English, The Stray Branch* and the indie book *In Between Spaces – Miami.* Currently, she is pursuing an MFA in Poetry at Saint Mary's College of California. Stella attended the Hedgebrook Writing Workshop and the Zelda Glazer Writing Institute. Santamaría performed spoken word in the Lab in San Francisco (2018) and in

New York City (2009) for the Ultimate Latina Festival at the Nuyorican Poets Café. She was interviewed for the CNN documentary (2010) *Latinos in America.*

PHUONG T. VUONG has been awarded fellowships from Tin House, VONA/Voices, and Kearny Street Workshop's Interdisciplinary Writers Lab. She has publications in or forthcoming in *Black Warrior Review, Cosmonauts Avenue,* The Asian American Writers' Workshop: *The Margins, Apogee,* and elsewhere. Her debut poetry collection *The House I Inherit* was released from Finishing Line Press in early 2019, and she is currently an MFA candidate at the University of Colorado Boulder.

SEAN WILLIAMSON is an M.F.A. writing student at Sarah Lawrence College. In 2009, he started the indie production house, World Wide Dirt. His feature debut, *Heavy Hands,* was an official selection to the 2013 Raindance Film Festival (London). Sean is a Wisconsin native but now lives in Queens with his partner and two sons. "I-80E" is his first published piece of fiction.

JOSHUA ZELESNICK'S poetry and political essays can be found or are forthcoming in various journals and magazines, among them *Jubilat, Word For/Word, Called Back Books, Mid-American Poetry Review, The New People, Labor Notes, Guacamole Lit Mag,* and *Counterpunch.* A chapbook, *Cherub Poems,* will be coming out from Bonfire Books this winter. He's fought some labor rights battles with fellow workers for adjunct professor equity throughout the Pittsburgh metro area, most notably at Duquesne University, where the administration still refuses to recognize a democratically elected union. He recently transitioned from teaching college to teaching Library for Pittsburgh Public Schools. He lives at Borland Garden, a co-housing community, in East Liberty with his partner and two young daughters, where, with friends, he helps run a living room reading and music series.

9 780997 397239